Lilac Skully and the Halloween Moon

Book #3
In The Supernatural Adventures
of Lilac Skully

D1559337

Lilac Skully and the Halloween Moon

AMY CESARI

1.
Ghost Pancakes

When Lilac awoke, she had no clue where she was. It certainly wasn't Skully Manor. It was small, plain, and beige. Sunlight streaked through the slatted blinds, illuminating the walls in strips of gold.

She remembered escaping from an ominous place by riding a spectral horse under the light of a bright moon. It felt like a dream. There'd been demons with flaming torches and a benevolent witch. She'd eaten pizza with living kids. And she'd met so many ghosts—some dark and terrible, but some had been kind.

The Blue Lady! Lilac recalled the figure of the luminous blue apparition, and sat straight up. She'd been dropped off there by the Blue Lady at the instruction of a cryptic note in the middle of the night.

The note! She scrambled out of bed towards her coat and rummaged through the pockets. There was

1

a crumpled piece of paper, and she unfolded it with shaking hands. It was real. In her father's unmistakable handwriting, it read,

My dearest Lilac,

Do not return home to Skully Manor under any circumstances. I have made arrangements for you to stay with the Mulligans until my release.

With any luck, just another couple of weeks.

Yours, Father.

She sighed and sat back on her knees. Now she remembered. She was at the Mulligans' house, acquaintances of her father. They were amateur paranormal investigators and part of the Ghost Guard. They were nice enough, but she barely knew them. She'd only met them once or twice before.

The Mulligans' place seemed the opposite of Lilac's home at Skully Manor, which was a dilapidated yet once opulently decorated Victorian. This room looked perfectly plain. Just like the Mulligans. All beige and sparse, with a small bed, a beige patchwork quilt, and a few beige things stored in beige boxes. That was it. It had a low ceiling, straight lines, and simple fixtures. Lilac recalled the tall ceilings of Skully Manor that slanted this way and that—so high up that she felt insignificant beneath them at times.

She looked at the perfectly plain boxes stacked in the corner. "Transceivers," one said, and "Paranormal Equipment—To Be Repaired," said the other. Well, at least that looked familiar. Her father was a professional paranormal researcher. Or he had been, until the ghost-hunting organization, Black, Black, and Gremory had kidnapped him.

Lilac lay on the carpet and stared at the ceiling. This was just weird. What was she supposed to do? She barely knew these people. What was she supposed to say? Just walk out there into the kitchen, and say, "Hello! Thank you for taking me in, as I am an odd and wayward child. Please feed me, I'm starving?!"

She gulped and tried to swallow as much air as she could to ward off the pang of hunger. She smelled something cooking. She was wearing brand-new purple pajamas with white kittens that the Mulligans had waiting for her on her arrival. They were incredibly cute. But if she dared to go out, what should she wear? Talking to near-strangers was going to be awkward enough. Doing so in pajamas would be even worse.

Lilac changed back into the clothes she had worn the night before, an old purple velvet dress that was too big, woolen tights with brown corduroy pants over them and black and white striped socks underneath. Her clothes smelled of sulfur and sweat, and the bottom of her pants were covered in smudges of dust and dirt. She sighed. Nope. It hadn't been a dream. The strange cloud of memories she awoke with had been real.

Lilac opened the bedroom door, then hesitated. She peered her head out into the hallway of the Mulligans' tiny house. The same funny beige carpet with brown swirls covered the entire floor. All of the walls were painted a dingy yellow-beige-white. She could hear the drone of the TV set and the clinking of cups or dishes in the other room. She shut the door quickly and took a deep breath. It smelled like pancakes. She opened the door again, and stepped out, following the sounds of life.

When she reached the doorway of the kitchen, her heart began to pound. She was just about to dart back into the bedroom when Sue Ann Mulligan turned around.

"Oh! Good morning, Lilac," she said with a bit of a startle, as Lilac was just standing there, staring at her wide-eyed. Sue was wearing her pajamas—a Christmas monkey motif—even though it was October.

Lilac tried to smile and say good morning or at least utter something, but no words came out. She looked down and nodded awkwardly in the doorway.

"Hey there, Lilac," another voice said. It was Bobby Joe Mulligan, who stepped out from the kitchen to greet her.

Lilac felt the panic of shyness melt over her like a wave. She froze again, knowing she should say something—anything—but couldn't find the words. He was just as plain as his wife, friendly enough though, tall with a bit of rotundness accentuated by his grey sweats. Lilac couldn't help but remember the time he'd been scratched by a poltergeist at Skully Manor, and she'd watched him run away, screaming in terror.

"We're glad you're here, Lilac," Sue Ann said to her, "We want you to feel at home, okay?"

Lilac nodded, even though there was no way she could ever feel at home or even slightly comfortable in this boxy house that wasn't hers.

"How about some pancakes?!" Bobby Joe called out enthusiastically.

Lilac's eyes lit up.

"Come into the kitchen," Sue Ann beckoned her from the doorway.

Bobby Joe swung his spatula around in the air.

"Bobby makes the best pancakes," Sue said to Lilac.

"They're blueberry! And I shape them like little ghosts!" Bobby called out playfully from the stove, waving his arms up in the air a bit. Sue Ann laughed.

Lilac couldn't help but giggle.

"I wonder if we have any chocolate chips?" Sue rummaged through the back of the cabinet. Lilac's stomach rumbled, and her mouth watered at the thought of chocolate chips.

"Aha!" Sue called out as she discovered half a bag of chocolate chips in the back of the pantry. "Have a seat over here, Lilac," she pulled out a chair at the kitchen table for Lilac, and Lilac sat down.

Lilac would have really liked some tea, but she didn't ask. She was also thirsty for water but just sat and waited. Sue gave Lilac a plate of blob-like ghost-shaped pancakes dyed a swirly blue from the blueberries. They had chocolate chips for eyes. Then Sue handed her a glass of orange juice. When Lilac saw the orange juice coming her way, she wanted to cheer. But she didn't. She tried to mumble out a thank you, and she was pretty sure Sue Ann heard her.

They all ate pancakes for a few minutes, Lilac silently, the other two commenting now and again how delicious they were. Lilac wanted to bring up her father and the Ghost Guard and kept thinking of different ways she could approach the subject as she ate.

Finally, Lilac spoke. "Um... last night you said... we could talk about my father and... the Blue Lady said the Ghost Guard has a plan to rescue him?"

"Oh," Sue said understandingly. "Yes, Lilac, but we don't want you to have to worry about any of that, okay? You've been through enough already, and you're safe here." She smiled, and Bobby nodded in agreement.

Lilac took another bite of pancake and thought carefully.

"But um... my dad's note said it would be a couple of weeks 'till he'd be home, do you really think it'll be that long, I mean..." Lilac searched for the words to say.

"Not to worry, Lilac," Bobby said. "We're involved with the Ghost Guard, as you know, and... you've gotta trust us. There is a plan in the works to rescue your father, believe me, it's been a big priority to rescue him and the Blue Lady..."

"But..." Lilac stammered. "I... I actually... rescued the Blue Lady, um... the other night?"

"Now, Lilac," Bobby Joe said, "let's just drop that subject for now and eat these delicious pancakes, huh? Let the Ghost Guard handle this one. We've got this."

Lilac's heart dropped. She was dying to know more about the Ghost Guard and the plans to rescue her father. It was of the utmost importance.

"Well, the Blue Lady said she'd come back to see me and tell me more in a couple nights anyway, so, maybe if you can just tell me what you know *now* instead...," Lilac tried to reason.

Sue sighed and smiled.

"You're just going to have to be patient here, okay?" Bobby said, then took a large bite of pancake, folding an entire half over and stuffing it into his mouth.

"Well, a couple weeks is a long time for me to be here. Do you think I could go visit my friends?" Lilac asked.

"No!" Bobby and Sue said back immediately at the exact same time, their mouths full.

Lilac looked back and forth between them. Her lower lip twisted. "They're the only *real* friends I've ever had," Lilac said. "In my entire life!" She forced herself to say it, although it hurt to admit it, and she barely got the words out. She swallowed the lump in her throat. "You can't deny a kid that." She shook her head and set her fork down next to a half-eaten ghost-shaped pancake. "I *have to* at least go see Hazel and Finn."

Sue and Bobby gave each other a look. Sue smiled a little and let out a laugh.

"Lilac," she replied, "You're safe here. There's a lot going on, and we're responsible for you. We can't take any chances. And if they're your *real friends*," she squinted one eye, "they'll understand."

Lilac's hands clenched under the table. In the worst case scenario, she'd lose Hazel and Finn and she'd never have real friends again, ever. But how could she explain that? They'd never understand the depths of her plight—hidden away in a haunted house for almost the entire nine-and-three-quarter years of her childhood. There was no way the Mulligans could grasp the importance of her budding friendship with Hazel and Finn. No way.

"What about my father?" Lilac asked again. "I want to join the Ghost Guard. I think it's only fair since..."

Bobby cut her off. "Lilac, please, we've discussed this."

Lilac prodded. "The Blue Lady told me that there's a plan to rescue him and all the ghosts, too. Well, I need to be a part of this. I can help, I swear!" She picked up her fork and knife again and took a large bite of ghost pancake, glaring and chewing intently as she waited for an answer.

"How often do you talk to ghosts, Lilac?" Sue asked her.

The way she phrased it made Lilac pause. She was just about to answer, "Every day," which was now true. But would they think she was strange?

"I... I don't know," Lilac stuttered in her response. "More lately, I guess. Why?!" Lilac asked, realizing they had changed the subject. "How long have *you* been involved with the Ghost Guard? And how often do *you* talk to ghosts?" She sliced the rest of the pancake quickly and dramatically.

There was an amused glance between the couple, and Sue responded. "We've been involved with the Ghost Guard for over two years now, I think with the recent developments, we're all hoping to make some real progress and wrap up our..."

"Well, I'm joining the Ghost Guard." Lilac cut in, waving her butter knife. "And that's final!"

The adults looked at each other and couldn't contain their laughter.

Lilac burned inside and shot back a cold stare. "Can I go get my cat?" she asked. "At least? And visit my *ghost* friends at home since I'm not allowed to see my *living* human friends?"

"At Skully Manor?" Sue Ann shook her head. "Lilac. Absolutely not."

Bobby Joe interrupted. "You're going to have to hang tight and just stay here for now. And *that's* final."

Lilac's forehead wrinkled and her eyes narrowed. She paused, then spoke. "But it's my cat!" She enunciated each word. "And the ghosts at Skully Manor aren't safe. I should be there protecting them!" she yelled as she stood up from the table.

Her heart was pounding, and all of her pale, thin limbs were shaking. Her stringy white-blonde hair was a mess, in tattered braids, uncombed and telling its own woeful tale of the past few days and frantic nights. Dark circles hung under her grayish, unblinking eyes, looping down in stark contrast to her unnaturally whitish skin. And she couldn't believe she was suddenly being so snappy. But it was like the force of raw life energy was flowing through her. She had nothing left to lose. It was like she was suddenly invincible.

"Calm down, Lilac," Sue tried to reassure her, "It's going to be okay, honey."

"Your cat will survive." Bobby said, much less soothingly.

Lilac scoffed and crossed her arms and tried to steady her trembling, the butter knife still in hand, pointed like a weapon.

"Explicit orders. From your father and the Ghost Guard, Lilac. You cannot go back to Skully Manor. It's being monitored, and it's the first place they'll be looking for you." Bobby added. "This is a big mission with a lot of moving parts, okay?" he added as he waved his hands around.

Lilac sneered and rolled her eyes. She said nothing else and tried not to eat another bite in a hunger strike, although she was still famished.

On one hand, she was very grateful to have the Mulligans take her in and feed her and give her purple kitty pajamas and a place to stay. But what did they expect of her? To sit by herself and wait for her father's rescue? To give up the first chance at real friends she'd ever had in her entire life?

Bobby and Sue ate their pancakes in an awkward air of silence. Lilac stared into the depths of the table. Bobby broke the silence by commenting again on how delicious the pancakes were. Lilac thought of six different things she could say in rebuttal, but said nothing. The smell of buttery pancakes overwhelmed her, and she resumed eating.

"So Lilac," Sue said, "it sounds like you've had some adventures the past few nights. Do you want to talk about it?"

Lilac froze, fork mid-air, her mouth stuffed. She looked suspiciously at Bobby Joe and Sue Ann. "What've you heard?" Lilac said abruptly and guiltily, as if that phrase were one word. "From who?" she added, her eyes shifting.

The adults exchanged a smirk and chuckled.

"Well," Sue glanced at Bobby and continued. "You said you had something to do with freeing the Blue Lady two nights ago."

Lilac continued chewing and raised just one eyebrow. Oh, she had something to do with it, alright.

"And... they said last night you... rode the... horse..." Bobby added, his face twisted a bit, nose wrinkled, his mouth barely able to say the words. "The one that pulls the legendary... um... Lost Souls Carriage?"

Lilac nodded, nonchalantly. Free a captured soul. Ride a ghost horse. All in a day's work for someone like Lilac Skully. Maybe two days, but still. She took another bite of pancake and didn't say anything else for a moment. They widened their eyes at her for further explanation, but she didn't give one.

She finished her pancake and unceremoniously stabbed another one off of the plate in the center of the table.

"Why were you... riding the horse?" Sue asked her.

"Oh well, I got kidnapped and brought to the Underworld." Lilac tried to explain. "And we escaped together. Titan and I. He's the horse."

The adults put their forks down. Their condescending chuckles had swiftly vanished and were replaced with an aura of impending doom.

"And a witch helped us, too. Cerridwen's her name. She's actually a very nice lady..." Lilac said as she nodded to herself.

"And how'd you get down there?" Bobby Joe asked after a few moments.

"To the Underworld?" Lilac asked.

He nodded.

She finished chewing. She set down her fork. She took a sip of delicious juice. "The carriage was hijacked, and... Titan couldn't help it, he got scared," Lilac tried to explain for the horse. "It really wasn't his fault."

"You rode... *inside* the Carriage of Lost Souls?" Bobby Joe asked, stuttering a bit.

Lilac nodded, just barely. Her eyes gazed between Bobby Joe and Sue Ann. Their faces seemed to have lost their color, and they looked uneasy about what she going to say next.

"And who did you see down there?" Bobby asked her. "Do you know who... brought you there?"

"Mr. Gremory," Lilac said plainly. "Or that's what he said his name was," She added. "I think it was him, though." She shrugged. "Gremory from Black, Black, and Gremory."

The adults looked at each other at the mention of his name. Bobby's eyes were trembling a bit. Sue Ann rubbed a chill off of her arms.

"I..." Lilac tried to explain, but she stopped talking.

"And *where* were you?" Sue Ann asked.

"The Un-der-world," Lilac said again very slowly, not sure if Sue hadn't heard her the first two times, or if she just didn't believe her. "That's what he told me, anyway. It's like a cave and..." Lilac tried to explain again, but when she saw the fearful, pitying, and otherwise conflicted range of expressions pass over both Bobby and Sue's faces, she stopped.

"How about some cartoons?" Sue offered a few moments after they had all finished eating. She shuffled Lilac to the TV room, turned the TV to a channel with cartoons, then left the room.

The cartoons played as Lilac's thoughts raced. If she could do what she wanted right now, she'd go straight to Hazel and Finn's house to return their scooter, even though she secretly hoped they'd let her borrow it for longer. Then once she was certain that Hazel and Finn weren't mad at her, she'd go to Skully Manor where she'd carefully sneak in the back door. She'd make sure the ghosts were okay. She'd get her cat. And the Blue Lady said she'd stop by Skully Manor to update the ghosts. Lilac's heart skipped a beat and she sat up. That meant the ghosts at Skully Manor probably had more information!

Over the sound of her own thoughts, she heard Sue and Bobby whispering in the other room. Lilac got up slowly and crept down the hall. She didn't think she'd be able to make out what they were saying, but when she cupped her ear to the door and concentrated real hard, she could hear them—just barely. They were talking about her.

"Do you think it's true? What she said about Gremory and the Underworld?" Sue asked. "I mean... this just confirms all the terrible things we've heard..."

her whisper was strained.

"I don't know, Sue." Bobby Joe sounded as if he was holding his hands over his face. "But if the rumors are true, if Gremory is actually a demon, a real live *demonic demon,* we're way out of our league here. Way."

Lilac's heart sunk. A demon. Out of their league. Great. This didn't sound promising at all. How were they going to help rescue her father with that kind of attitude?

"I feel so bad for her," Sue Ann added. "She's been through so much already." She paused, then continued. "Maybe it would be good for her to go see her friends, just for a little bit? She's going to get bored here by herself, for who knows how long..."

"No way," Bobby Joe responded. "She can't go anywhere. She's not our kid. We agreed to keep her safe, and we can't take any chances. They're already looking for her, and if Gremory is actually a *demon...*" he said again. The tone of his voice was unmistakable when he said it, a mix of confusion and horror. "A *demon!*" he exclaimed in a shocked whisper. "*Deee-mon!*" He dragged the word out one more time in a low, gravely voice, as if he were possessed.

"Then she won't be safe here for long, anyway," Sue said with a heavy sigh.

And with that, Lilac crept back to the TV.

2.
The Halloween Commercial

L ilac tried to watch the cartoon, a shameless rip-off of "Scooby Doo" called "Goober and the Ghost Chasers." But it didn't keep her attention.

She lay flat on the swirling brown and beige carpet, staring at the ceiling. The living room was just as plain as the bedroom and kitchen, all beige with a simple sofa, a small television set, a lamp, and a coffee table with absolutely nothing interesting on it.

She wondered what the ghosts at Skully Manor were doing right now. She wondered if they were haunting at all since she wasn't there. And she hoped that Archie was feeding Casper, as he said he would, otherwise she knew her cat would be very hungry by now.

Her thoughts of home were interrupted by spooky, bloopy, whistling sounds and music coming from the TV. She turned her head to the side to see what it was.

"Hey kids! Come on down to the Haunted Halloween

Carnival!" an animated skeleton spoke in a silly, echoey voice.

"Come trick or treat! Ride the rides! Candy apples! Corn dogs! Burgers and fries!" the skeleton said.

Lilac stared at the entrancing pictures on the TV screen—mouthwatering food, carnival rides, bright, colorful painted signs and games with hundreds of lights, and happy, joyful children all dressed up in magical costumes and masks.

"You'll have a spooky good time in our Haunted House! Scream with fright! Halloween delight! Come one, come all, little kiddies and get scared silly all night!"

For most of her life—due to the fact that she'd lived in a haunted house and was terrified of ghosts—Lilac would have steered clear of anything "haunted" or "spooky." That included Halloween and even TV shows like "Goober" and "Scooby Doo." But things had changed.

She continued to watch the advertisement. The masks and Halloween costumes didn't seem frightening and awful. In fact, it looked quite fun. She began to imagine herself in several costumes. What would she be? An Egyptian princess? A ghost? An animal, maybe a horse or a cat? Or what about a witch? Her eyes lit up, and Lilac began to imagine what she would look like in a pointed witch's hat and green makeup. Of course, the real witch she'd met just a few days before didn't wear that kind of hat or have green skin, but perhaps her costume could.

Lilac watched the images of happy children laughing as they collected huge sacks of delicious candy—riding on rides, screaming with joy and glee. She stared at the flashing lights, games, prizes, masks, candy apples, and just plain fun flowing through the air. Lilac could taste the candy. Taffy, she thought. Lots of taffy. Banana taffy. And a candy apple. Even though she'd never had a candy apple before, Lilac imagined how sweet and magnificent it would taste.

The skeleton reappeared on the screen. "This Halloween Night! Down at the Seaside Fun Park!"

"Lilac?" she heard over her shoulder, but she didn't respond, not wanting to leave the sweet trance of Halloween. The commercial ended. Lilac felt a sinking feeling of despair in her stomach. All she could do was hope the commercial would play again so she could experience it one more time and imagine what the magic of Halloween might really be like.

"You okay in here?" Sue asked.

Lilac turned her head the other way, towards the door, and nodded.

"Let me know if you need anything, okay?" Sue added.

"I need to go to the Seaside Fun Park for Halloween." Lilac said in a quiet, monotone voice, still laying flat on the floor.

Sue Ann burst out in a laugh. "Oh, Lilac." She shook her head. "What are we going to do with you?" And she left the room.

Lilac thought they should just let her do whatever she wanted. She didn't understand why that had to be so complicated.

She watched cartoons listlessly for several hours, dozing in and out of sleep. The Halloween advertisement played every twenty minutes or so, and by the afternoon, Lilac had seen it at least six or seven times.

She had two sandwiches for lunch, a glass of orange juice and six cookies. The day wore on, and after hours of daydreaming and watching TV, Lilac's eyes glazed over. Even the skeleton's now-familiar voice didn't give her the same rise as it had the first few times she saw it. She was at the point of feeling sure that she would never be able to experience Halloween as a child or wear a costume or have any fun, ever.

Lilac somehow managed to fall asleep for a proper nap on the sofa to pass the time, although she wasn't really tired anymore. She awoke to the sound of the skeleton's voice. Her eyes opened just a slit, and she watched the commercial sideways, half awake. Then something on the screen caught her eye. She jumped up and ran towards it.

"Was that..." she said and waited for the same scene to be played again, yet it didn't come back. But Lilac knew what she had seen. It was a ghost, riding on the carousel. And it wasn't a fake one like the rest of the Halloween decorations at the Fun Park. Lilac had a lot of experience with ghosts, whether she liked it or not. And she was sure she'd seen a real ghost in the Halloween commercial.

She waited impatiently through another round of TV for the commercial to come back again. And there she was. A woman on the carousel. It was blurry and she only came around twice, but Lilac could clearly make out the apparition dressed all in white with a large, wide-brimmed hat bobbing along to the motion of the horse.

Somehow she knew about that ghost. She'd read about it somewhere. Or someone had told her. Had it been a dream? Or something that Hazel and Finn told her about? Or the ghosts at Skully Manor?

"The notebook!" Lilac said under her breath. Her mother's notebook. That was it! She'd seen some notes about the haunted carousel. Lilac lay back on the floor and put her hands over her face. What did it say, though? She tried to imagine the page so she could read it in her mind. But it didn't work. She couldn't summon it in her head, and the notebook was in the drawer of her bedside table back at Skully Manor.

Lilac sat up and grasped her knees, curling into a ball. She had wanted to savor her mother's journal. Now she wished she had read it all at once. Then she'd know what it said already and she wouldn't have this terrible gnawing feeling of unknowing.

"What does it matter," she sighed. Her mother's notebook was older than she was. As much as she wanted to read it, it probably had nothing to do with anything going on now.

Lilac's rumbling stomach reminded her of her cat. She tried to send psychic messages to Archie, the little poltergeist, to remind him to put some food in Casper's bowl. She also hoped that he and the other ghosts of Skully Manor were okay, and it gave her a bit of a sick feeling inside. They weren't safe without her. Not if the men from Black, Black, and Gremory came back with their ghost-hunting equipment, anyway.

She lay back on the carpet and stared up at the ceiling. The homesickness she'd felt for Skully Manor had intensified to an unrelenting desire to go back. Just to check up on everything. Just for a couple of minutes. She reached into her pocket and unfolded her father's note. She read it again. "*Do not return home to Skully*

Manor under any circumstances," it said.

"Uuuugh." She rolled over onto her stomach. "And he doesn't think he'll be released for a couple of weeeeeeks." She sighed. "I just can't wait that long," she said. "I've got to go, just to check." She rolled onto her back again. "He'd agree with me if I could explain my reasoning..." she said of her father. "I'm sure of it."

And with that, she decided. She was going to sneak out tonight and go back to Skully Manor. As much as she wanted to see Hazel and Finn, the situation with her home, her ghosts, and her father was much more desperate.

Lilac dozed off again till Sue called her in for dinner. Lilac quietly ate three helpings of pasta with hamburger meat and cheese sauce. It was magnificently salty and delicious. Lilac tried to thank the Mulligans and be polite, but she couldn't think of anything else to say during the meal. All she could think of was her plan to escape.

She went to bed early and closed the door to the spare room, but she did not sleep. She waited impatiently for the Mulligans to go to bed, listening at the door for hours to the sound of their TV playing into the night.

Just after ten-thirty, she heard the TV click off.

"Well, let's get this over with. See what we're in for now." Lilac heard Bobby Joe mumble.

"Do you think she's asleep?" Sue Ann asked in what seemed like a fairly loud whisper.

"What does it matter?" Bobby said.

"What if she hears us?" Sue asked.

"We'll lock the door so she doesn't barge in," he replied.

Lilac rolled her eyes. Who did he think she was? Some kind of a snoop?

She heard the sound of their muffled steps as they walked down the carpeted hallway. A door shut. After waiting a few moments, as quietly as she could, Lilac stuck her head out into the hall. The doors to the bedroom and bathroom were open. There was only one place they could have gone— out into the garage.

She heard a faint but unmistakable sound come from behind the garage door. It was the sound of static over a radio.

Lilac crept closer. She could hear their muffled voices. She cupped her ear to the door, closed her eyes, and listened hard.

"Hello? Come in," she heard Bobby Joe's voice say, then the static continued till she heard a "beep," and another voice broke through.

Lilac gasped and covered her mouth to stifle the sound. It sounded like the gruff voice of Luther, the dark and gloomy ghost who was a member of the Ghost

Guard. A powerful and important member of the Guard at that, from what Lilac could tell.

"We're gonna make this quick." Luther's voice said over the radio. "Cancel all of your little plans for Halloween night, we've got an unexpected opportunity."

Lilac heard Bobby Joe sigh behind the door.

"Bet you didn't think this would be so much fun, did you?" Luther said sarcastically into the radio, not waiting for them to respond. He continued. "There's going to be a raid. At the roadhouse. Gremory's coming in to capture as many souls as possible with some new..." Luther's voice scoffed. "Equipment." He paused. "Whatever the hell kind of god-awful contraption he's got this time," he added with a sneer.

"What?" Lilac could hear Sue Ann whisper in what sounded like panic, not into the radio, but just to Bobby Joe.

"I... I don't think we can make it that night.... Um..." Bobby Joe stuttered into the radio in reply. "We do have... um... plans?"

"Nonsense." Luther shot back. "You signed up for this, and you're a part of it. Halloween night. We need you there."

"Are... are you sure?" Bobby Joe stuttered.

Luther's lengthy scoff mixed with the static of the radio came through thick, crackly, and irritated. "Look."

He said and inhaled deeply and audibly again, as if to keep himself from exploding from exposure to their ignorance. "Here's all you need to know. There's going to be a raid at the roadhouse where Gremory and gang are planning to capture a great many ghosts at once. And you, the Dynamic Duo, will be helping us to thwart their plans. What we're thinking is that if they see living humans in the building, it might distract them, at least enough for us to disable whatever slipshod ghost hunting equipment they roll up with next."

"You're going to send us in as decoys?" Bobby Joe said into the radio.

"Exactly right." Luther replied.

"Oh jeez!" Bobby Joe said to Sue Ann. "I think we're in way over our heads."

"Just calm down, Bobby, calm down..."

"Hello?" Luther's voice said again.

"Yeah." Bobby sighed.

"So... meet up at headquarters. Halloween. Six in the evening. And be ready for a long night." Luther added. "Over and out."

The radio beeped a final beep.

Lilac heard Bobby let out an exasperated sigh.

"What are we gonna do, Sue? They're sending us in as decoys... for a demon." He said.

Lilac was startled by the doorknob turning on the

door that her ear was plastered up against. She jumped backwards and scurried down the hall, shutting the door to her room just as Sue and Bobby emerged.

She listened again as they went into their bedroom, and exchanged a few moments of worried and hushed conversation that she could not hear.

Lilac waited for what seemed like an hour until she was pretty sure they were asleep. She turned the handle of the door, and it opened with a quiet click. She walked down the hall, the brown carpet padding her footsteps and cloaking her in silence.

The nice thing about a newer house like this, Lilac thought, was that the doors and hinges and floorboards don't squeak and squeal like the ancient, rusty doors and floors in Skully Manor. It made sneaking around so much easier.

She took a deep breath, unlocked the front door, and slipped out into the night.

3.
THE STATE OF SKULLY MANOR

Finally! She was free! The fall night air rushed through her lungs, and the frustration of her day lifted. Staying in the shadows, Lilac rode Hazel's little pink scooter back towards Skully Manor. It wasn't that far, about ten or twelve blocks towards the outskirts of town.

An owl hooted overhead, in time with her breath, now heavy and panting from the ride. She slowed down so she could approach the manor house as quietly as possible. She knew it might be monitored by Gremory's men, but at this point, she really didn't care. She'd dealt with them before, and she knew all the ins and outs of the house. She'd be fine.

Lilac approached the tall, crooked house from the front. It was three stories high with a tower in the middle. The dormer windows drooped down like sad eyes. And the tangled brambles of the garden reached up and out in every direction, as if they were trying to escape.

She crouched down and peered at the house from around the back of a large station wagon. There were no signs of the white surveillance vans. The neighborhood was still and quiet. Lilac circled around the block, slipping from shadow to shadow, waiting until she was absolutely certain that there were no signs of Gremory's henchmen. Then she snuck through the back gate of Skully Manor.

"Mrooooow!" she heard, and jolted back with a gasp.

"Casper, shhh!" She picked up her sandy white striped cat and shushed him. "It's good to see you!" she whispered.

He quieted down, purring happily in her arms. She descended the cold, damp stairs and slipped through the cellar door, still hanging crookedly off of one busted hinge from the first time Black, Black, and Gremory broke in.

The basement was pitch black. She set her cat down.

"Milly?" She whispered. "Bram?" She put her hands out in front of her. Stumbling through the darkness, Lilac found the first light. She pulled the string. The dim bulb flickered. The basement looked pretty much as she'd left it. Lilac continued up the stairs that led to the main floor. Each step creaked as she walked, and she tripped a bit as Casper followed along under her feet.

"Milly?" Lilac whispered again. Casper jumped nimbly through the hole that the henchmen had punched through the door with the candlestick, and Lilac followed.

The foyer was dark.

"Bram?" She called. "Archie?"

"Liii-lac!" a familiar voice whispered.

"Milly!" Lilac said in delight as the apparition of the little girl ghost swooped down to greet her. "Archie!" She called out as Milly's little brother followed down not far behind. They both had a blue glow, and wore neatly tailored Victorian party wear. Milly had on a lace-trimmed dress with a gigantic droopy bow in her hair, while Archie wore a tidy sailor suit, cap, and saddle shoes.

"We've got to be quiet. Bram says they might still be listening. You never know!" Milly said. "It's so good to see you! We've got so much to tell you. Those terrible men have been back! They didn't come for us, but they were here. Only briefly, but... oh, we've been so worried about you since we saw you from the window!"

"I missed you guys, and I've been so worried about you too." Lilac said. "Um, but didn't the Blue Lady come to tell you I was alright?" Lilac asked. The Blue Lady had told her she would stop by Skully Manor to update the ghosts. If Lilac recalled correctly, the Blue Lady had said that twice.

"The Blue Lady?" Milly gasped in shock. "But she's been captured for ages!"

"I freed her!" Lilac exclaimed, till she was shushed by another familiar voice.

"Miss Skully," Bram said, "some of the immediate danger here has passed, but, please, keep it down. And don't turn on any more lights. In fact, turn those off in the cellar."

"Hi Bram!" Lilac whispered to the ghost butler, dressed as he always was, ready in uniform, a crisp black suit with vest and tails.

Milly shut off all the lights as she was skilled to do with her otherworldly talents.

"Wonderful to see you're alright, Lilac. Now, what was that you said? You freed the Blue Lady?!" Bram whispered.

"Well, yes!" Lilac recounted, as quietly as she could, explaining what they had missed and how she ended up at the Mulligans' house last night.

"Unbelievable." Bram seemed astonished. "That's incredible, Lilac, well done!"

Archie and Milly stared at her in amazement.

Lilac beamed. But then her smile faded. "So, Blue didn't come here to tell you I was okay?" Lilac asked again. She scrambled to understand. Why would Blue tell her that and then not do it?

"No," Bram said. "But perhaps she felt it wasn't safe to do so with the surveillance vans and some of the activity the past couple days. After all, she was kidnapped out in the garden, I'm sure they'd look for her there again. In fact, now that I think about it, I believe that's probably why they were here. They were looking for her." He nodded. His reasoning made it all sound logical.

"Well, where do you think I can find her again?" Lilac asked. "The roadhouse, I guess?"

"Oh, Miss Skully," Bram said. "Please. It's far too dangerous for you to be involved in this. Why, it sounds like things are worse than we could've imagined. It's best you go right back to the safe house where you were placed and…"

"I've *got* to find Blue," Lilac said as she folded her arms. "She's involved with the ghosts that are gonna rescue my father! She's the only one that'll tell me anything about him. Besides, I want to ask her if I can help with the Ghost Guard's mission." Her eyes widened. "Gremory is planning a big capture of ghosts just down the street at the roadhouse. Soon! On Halloween! I just found out about it tonight when I snooped on the Mulligans, I think they were talking to that ghost named

Luther on some kind of radio," Lilac said, as if she had some very important information to share.

"Luther." Bram said the name like it smelled bad, and rubbed his forehead a bit. "Oh, Lilac, please promise me you won't get any further involved in this. Please." He pleaded.

"Wait, I think we heard them talking about that when they snuck in here the other night. Did you hear them, Milly?" Archie said to his sister. "They were in your father's lab, Lilac, the ghost hunters. They were looking for something. But I don't think they took anything."

"Well, I don't know what they *said*," Milly scoffed. "I was too terrified that they were going to try to capture me in one of those horrible orbs."

Lilac looked at Bram.

"I heard nothing of the sort," he said. "But you must leave right away, Lilac. It's not safe here."

Lilac's heart began to pound a bit, thinking about how vulnerable they were right now, in a pitch black, unsecured manor house that had been targeted by a series of break-ins, ghostnappings, and other nefarious plots masterminded by an organization of evil ghost hunters. They could be out there right now. Listening. Or about to come in the front door. Or the back. Or they could already be upstairs. One of the men might've seen her creep through the garden gate. If they came in now, she would be trapped. Her father had said not to return under any circumstances. But she did anyway. She took a deep breath.

"Well I guess I have to leave pretty soon," she said. "But first I want to get my mom's notebook. And I might take Casper back with me, just so he doesn't get lonely, um... not that you guys aren't good company," she tried to explain to the ghosts as to not be rude, "But um, he and I are best friends, you know, he needs... me..."

"Perfectly fine, Miss Skully, " Bram said. "Hurry it up then, get your things and go, don't dally here too long. And don't worry about us. We're fine here. The children and I have haunted this manor for over one hundred years. Lord knows we are capable on our own."

But Lilac knew that wasn't true. They needed her protection. She went upstairs to her room, the dark manor lit only by the moon and stars.

She fumbled through her bedside drawer and took out her mother's notebook. She brought it over to the faint light of the window and flipped through the pages.

"Here!" she said. "The haunted carousel! That's what I was looking for..."

"Miss Skully," Bram said, as the ghosts had all followed her up. "Please take it and read it once you've returned to the safe house."

"Oh!" Lilac gave a small yelp. "I… I can't believe it… "
She covered her mouth, her eyes enormously wide.

"What!" Milly asked as she and Archie floated
towards her.

"That's today's exact month and day, but written
many years ago, how very… strange," Lilac said and
shuddered a bit.

Lilac began to read the passage that her mother
wrote. It felt like she was reading from a book of magic.
Time stood still, her heart thumped, and she read it
slowly and carefully, taking in each beautifully written
word.

*"And I'm looking forward to Halloween night, a group of
us are going to the Seaside Fun Park. We've got permission
to run an investigation and set up our equipment at the old
Haunted Carousel."*

Lilac got goosebumps. She continued to read.

*"Folklore has it that Halloween is the time when the veil
between the world of the living and the world of the spirits is
at its thinnest,"*

Lilac stopped to take a couple of deep breaths
through her mouth to steady herself, and set one hand

over her heart. Then she read more.

So, Marvin and James got the idea to investigate on Halloween, to increase our chances of seeing ghosts!

Marvin and I are interested in the Carousel Ghost because of our research with the Lady in the Lighthouse and the possible connection between the two. The Lighthouse Ghost is, of course, most famous for sinking ships with lightning, but another legend has it that she and her sister are ghosts locked in a perpetual argument, even in death.

The next part of our investigation is to follow some of the leads on who this mysterious sister is, and if she still haunts. The most widely known theory is that her sister is the woman on the carousel—many even take it as fact, however, no evidence or link has yet to be proven or disproven, other than both ghosts are typically seen dressed in white, and haunt in relatively close proximity to each other. So with any luck we'll pick up some evidence of the ghost on the carousel... and possibly find out if she had a sister!

Exciting stuff, but lots of tedious planning and work is going into this investigation. We're hoping it will score us some accolades and press to further fund our research. If we are able to record anything credible, that is. And if things go as swimmingly as they have been, I think luck is in our favor!

Oh, and another fascinating ghostly tidbit of local lore and legend—it's said that when the Full Moon falls on Halloween, hundreds of spirits rise and gather along the beach, right at the Seaside Fun Park. There's a bit of a debate amongst local paranormal investigators as to if these occurrences happen every Halloween, or only when the moon is full on Halloween. Sadly, a full moon on Halloween only occurs every 18 to 19 years, so it's a mystery that proves to be a bit difficult to investigate with any frequency. And unfortunately the moon won't be full for us this Halloween. That won't happen for another 13 years! And you'd better believe Marvin and I will be there to investigate on the next Halloween Full Moon! We already have some amazing plans and ideas, it'll be a dream come true when that night finally comes.

There are so many exciting opportunities and things happening. I feel like we are truly a part of the paranormal community, and our dedication to researching the often misunderstood world of spirits and ghosts is paying off.

-Lenore.

Lilac stopped reading. "A dream come true," she said ever so softly. "She never got to do it." She swallowed. "And probably so many other things she wanted to do that she never did." She paused, then re-read the entry.

"The full moon won't happen on Halloween for thirteen years." Lilac said. "Ten," she counted up from the entry date. "Eleven. Twelve. Thirteen." She added till she got to the current year. "That's this year!" She said under her breath. "The full moon on Halloween is this year! *Exactly* thirteen years later!" She had to sit down cross-legged on the floor and hold her head in her hands. Then she hugged the notebook.

"*That's* what they were talking about!" Archie said. "When the ghost hunters came back in yesterday, they were talking about the full moon for sure. One of them said they thought it was a bunch of phooey. Well, they didn't use *that* word, but I'm not supposed to say the word they used. They were talking about capturing ghosts at the Seaside Fun Park, under the full moon on Halloween!"

"At the Fun Park?" Lilac asked. "But I overheard the Ghost Guard, and they said Gremory was capturing ghosts at the roadhouse because there are so many ghosts that go there."

"No," Archie shook his head firmly and a fine ethereal dust shook around him. " I know I heard 'em right. The men said it was the Gathering of the Ghosts at the Seaside Fun Park. And they were gonna capture all the ghosts there. I'm sure of it. It sounded terrible. And you just read the same thing about the full moon in your mom's diary."

It was true, her mother's notebook said something similar, although it had been written thirteen years ago.

Lilac re-read the entry one more time. The Carousel

Ghost. The Halloween Full Moon. Her mom's dream to be there.

She had to go to the Fun Park on Halloween. And if the Ghost Guard wouldn't listen to what Archie said, maybe she could stop Gremory's Fun Park plan on her own. She'd be there anyway, honoring her mother. There was no way she wasn't going. All signs pointed to the Fun Park on Halloween night. She had to go. Even if it meant sneaking out again.

"Well, I've got to go alert the Ghost Guard about the Fun Park and tell them what you heard." Lilac said. "I'm going to try to find Blue. She's the only one that might listen to me."

"The Ghost Guard?" Milly said in recognition. "Oh, that's what I heard them talking about! The bad men said they were on to them! It was a trap and they were leading the Ghost Guard to the roadhouse."

"A trap? For the Ghost Guard?" Lilac said with wide eyes.

"Yes, that's exactly what they said. They said they had plans to trap them all, and it frightened me away. I can't stand those awful ghost traps!" Milly said with a shiver.

Bram sighed. "Please just go and alert the living that you are staying with. Just tell them, Lilac, and get to safety. And stay there, please? At the safe house."

Lilac sighed and rolled her eyes. She rummaged through her closet for some kind of bag to carry her cat in. She took an old lucky crystal medallion out of her wooden treasure box and put it in her coat pocket. She pocketed the only bits of money she had, a few folded bills and some spare change.

"Lilac, please," Bram said again.

But Lilac did not listen. She rummaged through the kitchen drawers for a flashlight and some sort of pocketknife, but she didn't find anything. She packed up some cat kibble and scooped up her cat, placing him into a messenger bag, much to his dislike. She zipped the zipper just enough so his head stuck out. It would have to do.

"You've got to come with me, and we'll pretend you found me, okay? You followed my scent and showed up at the Mulligans' door," She whispered to the cat. "Now, be quiet."

He agreed.

Lilac said sweet goodbyes to her ghostly friends, with promises all around for everyone to be safe. She crept back down the musty basement stairs, making her way through the pitch blackness and the deathly still air of the manor basement.

When the scent of nettles and overgrown herbs in the garden hit her lungs, Lilac took a long, deep breath that only the living take. She carefully mounted her scooter and adjusted the bag so Casper was secure. She turned right at the side of Skully Manor, the silhouettes of the tombs and larger graves of the cemetery already visible ahead under the light of the nearly full moon.

Lilac approached the old cemetery from the shadows. When all seemed still and quiet, she snuck into the courtyard and hid behind the fountain as she had done the first time she staked out the roadhouse, a couple of nights ago.

She hoped she'd see Cerridwen the witch again. She'd seen her in this cemetery once before. Lilac wasn't quite sure how or why Cerridwen was associated with the ghosts, other than she rode in the Carriage of Lost Souls, too. But Lilac had really liked the old witch and felt like they might be friends now. And Cerridwen had called out, "See you around, little witch!" to Lilac as she flew off on a broom. *A broom!* Lilac closed her eyes for a moment and smiled warmly. She was more than a little giddy at this magical memory, although it seemed unreal. Maybe that part had been a dream. She listened carefully to pick out the low, grumbling tones of the witch's voice. But she didn't hear it.

"Blue?" Lilac whispered into the air. "Blue?" she said again.

It was a long shot, but Blue had once told Lilac to

meet her in this cemetery. Yet Blue didn't show up that night, Lilac recalled. And Blue had said she was going to tell the ghosts of Skully Manor that Lilac was safe. Twice. But she didn't tell them. Not once. Lilac didn't call out her name again.

She waited in the dark shadows, silently, just twenty yards or so from the old haunted roadhouse.

"Mrow?" Casper let out a quiet complaint.

"Shhh!" Lilac said. "We'll get out of here soon."

They waited for a while but saw no spirits. Lilac skirted back out of the cemetery and over to the shrubbery on the side of the road. From here, she could see the back door of the roadhouse. Maybe she'd see a soul she knew from this vantage point, like the Blue Lady or Luther or even Stewart the carriage driver.

She waited a little longer.

"Mrow?" Casper asked again about eight minutes later. Lilac knew that he was being as patient as he could, but he still wanted to know how long he'd be zipped in a bag.

"Just a couple more minutes," Lilac said under her breath.

When she was about to get up and go back to the Mulligans', the door of the roadhouse swung open.

Luther's massive dark figure stepped out. He was unmistakable in black robes, the fabric like velvet from another galaxy, so dark it might suck you in. Yet he glittered—ever so dramatically—dripping with thick ropey chains, jewels, ancient amulets, rings, and bracelets that twisted up his arms. His voice carried through the night, or at least it carried to Lilac's ears, which seemed to pick up the sounds of ghosts more than most.

Just as she was about to pop out of the shrubs to tell him what she had learned about the Seaside Fun Park and the trap for the Ghost Guard, Lilac gasped and shuddered back.

Christopher Stefengraph followed him out the door. He was the ghost that had helped kidnap her to the Underworld. He was jabbering about something that Lilac could not yet make out.

Luther sighed and crossed his arms. He looked out across the road, right where Lilac was hidden, and held his gaze. Lilac held her breath.

"Just make *sure* to have the gang ready here at the roadhouse, yeah?" she heard Christopher say to Luther.

Her stomach dropped. Luther said nothing.

"Well anytime you need my, shall we say, assistance, Luther, I'm glad to help. G'night, and good luck." Christopher tipped his hat to Luther and floated quietly down the road, fading out into the dark shadows of nothingness.

Lilac's mind raced. Christopher had been working with Gremory! Didn't Luther know that? It was so obvious. Blue must've told him that. Lilac might've even told him that herself. Something here didn't add up. Lilac began to shiver as a cold breeze blew through.

Luther's gaze had still not shifted, it held tight, right into the bushes where Lilac was crouched, as if he were thinking.

Lilac wanted to close her eyes, but she could not. All of the hairs on her arms stood up at once.

"Get out of here, Skully," Luther said in a voice she could barely hear.

"But I have to tell you something!" She shouted, much higher and more childish than she was expecting her voice to be. "It's a trap! You have the wrong information! Gremory's ghost raid is at the Fun Park! And Christopher is..."

"Out!" He said again, with such force that a gust of wind knocked her back.

Casper let out a scream from the bag, and Lilac gasped in panic. She heard Luther groan and chuckle a bit.

"Of course she's got a bloody cat in a bag with her now," he muttered. "Lord." He scoffed.

Her face burned with embarrassment. She managed to load herself and her cat back up onto the scooter, and with a massive thump of her heart and a ghostly tailwind from Luther pushing her doggedly down the alley, she went back towards the Mulligans' house.

4.

A Cat and a Witch Hat

Casper sniffed around the Mulligans' spare bedroom, settled down on the hand-stitched quilt, and went right to sleep. But sleep was nowhere to be found for Lilac.

If she told the Mulligans that Gremory's ghost raid was going to be at the Fun Park, not the haunted roadhouse, she'd have to confess that she had snuck out to Skully Manor. Yet if she didn't tell them, the Ghost Guard—including the Mulligans—would be walking into a trap, and they were the only hope she had to rescue her father. Unless she did it all herself.

But if she didn't tell the Mulligans, lives were at stake—living and dead. She had to tell them. Maybe if she was able to save the day with this information, they'd let her join the Ghost Guard. And then they could thwart Gremory together at the Fun Park on Halloween, and she could honor her mother, too. Yes! This was perfect. Then they'd come up with a plan to rescue her father, and she'd go back home. Everything would be fine.

When she realized that this might come together nicely after all, Lilac dozed off into a peaceful slumber.

"Aaaaachooo!"

Lilac was awakened from the kind of deep, desperately needed sleep where it's painful to open your eyes, and your head feels like a vise is tightening around it.

"Aaaaaachooo!" She heard again.

Lilac put the pillow over her head and tried to go back to sleep.

"Aaaaa.... Choooo!"

She heard the sneeze again, followed by some rather off-putting moaning and wailing from the hall outside the door.

"Aaaah! Why are my allergies acting up? Aaaaaa-choo!" Lilac heard Bobby moan from the bathroom on the other side of the hall, accompanied by the rattle of someone rummaging through drawers and cabinets.

"Aaa-chooooo! This hasn't happened since we went to your Aunt Clara's house with the cats and... Aaaa... Chooo!"

Lilac sat up. Casper's head perked up from the foot

of the bed, and he and Lilac exchanged a glance.

"Sue? Have you seen the allergy medicine?" Lilac heard Bobby call out.

The sureness of Lilac's late night plan was washed away with the day's first wave of doubt.

"Well," she said to Casper, "we might as well get this over with."

Besides, they smelled bacon.

Once dressed, Lilac crept in quietly and sat at the table.

"Good morning, Lilac!" Sue Ann said. "I hope you slept well."

"Well," Lilac said calmly, "no, I barely slept, because actually, I snuck out last night, and..."

"Aaaa-chooo!" Bobby came into the kitchen, holding a roll of toilet paper and a box of allergy tablets. "I just did the nasal spray," Bobby said with a sniffle. "It should help a lot."

"Mrow!" Casper said with confidence as he strode into the room.

"What?" Bobby exclaimed. "Where did this cat come from?"

Casper walked over to Lilac and jumped onto her lap.

Lilac smiled. It was a guilty smile, but it was a smile.

"Bobby Joe and Sue Ann, this is Casper, my cat. And Casper, this is Bobby Joe and Sue Ann Mulligan, friends of my father..."

Bobby Joe almost began to chuckle.

Lilac couldn't tell if he was really laughing because he thought it was funny or if it was an angry, evil laugh. He sneezed again, and then Sue Ann began to laugh a little, too.

"You're kidding me!" Bobby said, obviously flustered, yet unable to hide a twinge of amusement as he blew his nose. He turned his head dramatically to Sue, who was shaking her head and smiling gently.

"Nope!" Lilac continued. "Not kidding. As you can see by my cat. And guess what, you're actually going to be glad I did this because I found out some really important information from the ghosts at Skully Manor. The whole thing's a set-up! Archie and Milly overheard the men from Gremory talking about it. Since it's a full moon on Halloween, they're trying to lure the Ghost Guard into a trap at the roadhouse while they capture all the ghosts at the Fun Park!" She tried to explain it as succinctly and logically as she could, but the words sounded silly and jumbled and childish as she said them.

"Who told you this?" Sue Ann asked.

"Milly and Archie, the little girl ghost and her brother at my house. You know, they're sort of famous as far as ghosts go in this town..." Lilac said, trying to lend some credibility to her story.

They stared at her, kind of like she was crazy, and kind of like they were terrified.

Lilac tried to explain again. "The men from Gremory broke into my house again, and the ghosts overheard them talking about their plans." She said as seriously as she could. "You have to believe me and tell Blue or contact Luther on that radio thing again because I tried to tell him at the haunted roadhouse last night and..."

"Lilac!" Bobby Joe scolded. "Have you been listening in on us? And Luther? You were out trying to find that guy? Do you realize how dangerous your little late night mission was?"

"Um.... I... " Lilac sighed and paused as her heart began to beat very fast. "Look, I just happen to care. A lot. Okay? My father's been kidnapped by Gremory, and the Ghost Guard is his only shot at getting out. Other than me." She narrowed her eyes at them, expecting that they'd shush her or rebut with the maddening, circular logic of adults, but they did not.

"If the Ghost Guard walks into a trap at the roadhouse and they're all captured, then my father will really be doomed." She added. "Who knows what'll happen to him." She sat back in the chair and crossed her arms. "All the ghosts at the Fun Park will be captured, too! And it's putting you in danger! You should care about this. You're a part of it. Even if there's just a slight chance that the Ghost Guard is wrong, it should be looked into." Lilac's heart was thumping, and she was shaking by the time she was done speaking.

Bobby Joe and Sue Ann were silent. They looked at each other uncomfortably as Sue set a plate of bacon on the table. No one touched it.

"Will you at least try to tell someone else in the Ghost Guard?" Lilac said slowly, each word one at a time. It was the only way she felt like she could get the words out without exploding.

"Okay," Bobby said in a shaky voice. "Okay. We'll tell them if we can. But this... spying on us and sneaking out... has got to stop, Lilac. Seriously."

Lilac said nothing.

Sue poured Lilac a glass of orange juice, and Bobby began to eat some of the bacon.

"So?" Sue said a couple of awkward minutes later. "Bobby, should we tell Lilac about this afternoon?"

"Are you sure that's still such a good idea?" He said in a flat tone, blowing his runny nose again and not looking up.

"Lilac," Sue continued. "I'm hoping to drop you off with your friends for about an hour or so this afternoon, if they're home that is. What are their names? Amber and Quinn?"

Lilac looked between them incredulously.

"Hazel and Finn?" she said. "But... but you said I couldn't!"

"We know, but I've got an errand this afternoon and Bobby's going to be at work, so we thought maybe to keep you out of trouble..."

"If that's even possible!" Bobby said as he shook his head.

"Yes!" Lilac exclaimed "Oh yes that's amazing! Thank you! I swear I won't get into any trouble ever, ever, again and..."

"Well, if they're not home, you're going to have to come with me and hide in the back seat of the car, understand?" Sue said.

"Anything!" Lilac said. "Um... thank you!"

Lilac felt like fireflies were flittering in her stomach. She was going to see Hazel and Finn! It was a miracle.

She watched cartoons, waiting impatiently for the commercial breaks and the advertisement for the Halloween Carnival at the Seaside Fun Park. And there she was again. The Ghost on the Carousel. Riding a white horse with angel wings. Only this time it meant so much more, knowing the significance of this particular ghost to her mother.

Lilac went back to the sparse spare bedroom and pulled out her mother's notebook, curious to see if there were any notes about how the carousel investigation turned out. She found a terribly disappointing passage, lamenting that the whole thing had been called off by rain and flooding at the park that Halloween night. She covered her eyes and felt her mother's frustration for a few moments. Then she scanned through more pages of the notebook, trying to find anything else about the carousel or the Fun Park at a later date, but there wasn't anything. She closed the notebook and lay back on the bed to think. Casper jumped up on her lap and she pet him. He began to purr.

She rolled onto her side and read her mother's notebook again. It flipped itself open to a page written in a handwriting that looked a little messier, quicker, and more rushed than the beautiful script of her mother's other musings.

Lilac began to read it.

Home alone tonight, finally have some time to write a bit. Marvin is out with James, unfortunately. I hate to say that, and I've told Marvin I didn't want him to go. But he thought it might be a good idea to "patch things up" with James. Hmph. James is the one who should be patching things up, making an effort to apologize to us!

And even if he did, I don't think I would accept it. I'm so very.... vexed with James right now, I can't even stand it. He tried to take credit for all of the research that Marvin and I have been doing at the Lighthouse to the Paranormal Times! Yes, all of the credit. For research he isn't even doing or a part of! He just happened to be invited over to dinner and Marvin told him about some of it. I was furious when I found out. I knew he had been jealous, but this is just a betrayal of our friendship.

I'm really gossiping now (thankfully, no one will ever read this! If you are reading this, you shouldn't be! Tsk, Tsk!) but James just hasn't been the same since he and his brother, Solomon Black, have started working together. I guess his brother has a fascination with demons, summoning them and the like.

And Marvin and I have had to tell them now—twice—that we aren't interested in joining their research. While demonology can be considered an acceptable academic field of study in the paranormal community under the right circumstances—there's just something about him that seems... off. Unkind.

And there's this other man that they have been working with and bringing around to some of the paranormal council meetings and such. Gregory, or Gremory? Something like that, and I can't put my finger on it, but it's just been... well, strange. And uncomfortable. He knows too much. I've only been introduced to him once, yet he cornered me the other night at the awards banquet when I was coming back from *the restroom and said...*

Her mother's writing trailed off and did not pick back up again on the page.

Lilac flipped to the next page and there was a date several days later. She scanned the entry and it didn't mention anything about Gremory or what he had said to her. She flipped through a few more pages and didn't see anything else about it, either.

Lilac shut the notebook. She felt cold, and snuggled up under the hand-stitched patchwork quit on the bed, and hugged her cat close.

"My mom knew Gremory." Lilac said ever so quietly to Casper. "And Black. And... Black..." she said of the brothers. "And she didn't trust them." It sounded like her mom was starting to feel afraid. Or at least very uncomfortable.

And now her mother was gone, yet Lilac and her father Marvin were still dealing with the jealous, unkind men at Black, Black, and Gremory. Worse, she had a creepy feeling that would not go away. A feeling that they had something to do with her mother's death.

"An accident" was all her father ever managed to say about it. Lilac didn't know what that meant for a long time, until bits she'd heard from other people came together and she realized her mother had died somewhere in their house. In an accident.

It was as if a trail of dark smoke began to fill Lilac's lungs, each breath bringing her farther into the depths of a twisted web woven long before she was born. The men of Black, Black, and Gremory were her greatest foe. Her family's greatest foe. And she felt almost helpless against them. Almost.

The entry in the journal about her parents and Black, Black, and Gremory felt as dooming as it was depressing. Yet, as the afternoon went on, Lilac let herself fall back into the excitement of going to see Hazel and Finn. She was a little bit nervous, she admitted to herself.

Lilac watched TV for several more hours, until her mind melted into ennui once the dramatic adult TV shows came on in the middle of the day. Lilac tried to entertain herself as the minutes ticked by. Her head raced and bounced with haunted thoughts. The Ghost Guard. The ghost on the Carousel. The ghosts at her house. Ghosts, ghosts, ghosts.

Lilac almost jumped out of her skin when she heard the sound of Sue Ann calling her to go. She had been ready for hours, her boots and coat on, her hair brushed and freshly braided as best she could to make sure she didn't look too scruffy.

Sue Ann made Lilac wait inside while she checked

to make sure no one was watching them. Lilac waited, and then Sue came back and motioned Lilac to get into a small, beat-up white car that was parked out front.

Lilac pulled her hood up and scooted down a little bit, hoping to stay unseen. She then directed Sue, with a few wrong turns, until they arrived at the house of Hazel and Finn Cross.

As Sue was parking, Lilac blurted out, "They think my father has the flu. They don't know anything about the ghosts or his kidnapping or anything." She held her breath and waited for a response.

"Okay," Sue Ann looked at her with a wink. "And I'm your cousin, you're staying with us for a while till he gets better,"

Lilac nodded in agreement. She got out of the car and tried to walk calmly down the driveway, but started to run instead. She could hear the TV blaring in the twins' clubhouse in the back.

"Hazel and Finn are in there," Lilac said back to Sue and pointed to the rickety little garage. "And their mom, Patricia, is in the house," she pointed to the house. "I think," Lilac added.

"I'll go introduce myself to their mom," Sue said and motioned towards the door, "as your cousin." She winked again, and Lilac winked back.

Lilac suddenly felt very nervous. She gasped. She

had forgotten the scooter! It was still at the Mulligans'. Well, at least she could tell them she'd give it back soon.

"Lilac!"

An ecstatic voice startled Lilac out of her anxious trance. It was Hazel.

"I thought I heard someone out here! What, are you just going to stand outside? Come in!" Hazel laughed and ran back in. "Finn, it's Lilac!" She announced to her brother. "Come in here, Lilac,"

Finn barely looked up form the TV when she entered.

"Hey, Skully!" he said, munching on a bowl of popcorn and drinking a grape soda.

"Mom got grape," Hazel said excitedly, and handed a soda to Lilac.

"Th... thanks!" Lilac accepted it gladly, and looked back and forth between Hazel and Finn, trying to figure out what they were thinking and what she should say next. They didn't seem to be mad at all. They didn't even seem to notice that she had disappeared with the scooter. And she was overjoyed at seeing both of them—their matching dirty blonde shag hairdos, hazel eyes, and mischievous grins permanently plastered underneath freckled twin noses.

"Um..." Lilac said after she'd had a few sips of the grape soda, "I still have your scooter at my cousin's house and um... I'm really sorry I left... I..." she stumbled to find more words.

"Oh," Hazel said with wide, innocent eyes, shaking her head back and forth. "It's totally fine, we don't ride that scooter, you can keep borrowing it and..." Hazel seemed sort of at a loss for words. "Mom was a little worried about you," she admitted, "But we just told her..." Hazel stopped and looked down. She looked back up with a guilty, yet sweet smile. "We told her you were a little weird?" Hazel laughed.

Finn agreed by giving a grunting laugh.

Lilac suddenly felt much better. Things were looking good, like they were her real friends, after all. And even better, they were okay with her being a little weird. This was fantastic news.

"Sit down!" Hazel instructed, and Lilac took a seat on the big tufted and fringed turquoise chair.

The cartoon on the TV ended, and the advertisement for the Halloween Carnival at the Seaside Fun Park came on.

"Halloween!" Hazel and Finn shouted together. They seemed just as excited about it as Lilac had been.

"Come with us, Lilac!" Hazel screamed. "Oh you HAVE to!" She demanded.

"I... I don't know if I can... And I don't have a costume..." Lilac stammered. She didn't say how very badly she wanted to go. She also noticed that Hazel and

Finn hadn't mentioned the ghost in the commercial. She wondered if they were able to see ghosts, or if it was just her.

"You have to go!" Hazel implored. "It's your right! And you can wear one of my old costumes!" Hazel ran to a trunk in the back of the garage and started pulling things out. "I'm serious, Lilac. You have to come with us."

"I'm going to be Frankenstein's Monster!" Finn told Lilac. He grabbed a mask off the table and threw it over his head.

Lilac laughed. It was a pretty scary mask, but it was also funny to see Finn wearing it and waving his arms in jerky motions.

"I'm going as a cowgirl this year!" Hazel exclaimed, holding up her own costume for Lilac to see.

"Oh, that's so cool," Lilac said with wonder.

Hazel's cowgirl costume was incredible. It had a pink-and-purple cowgirl hat and matching boots. There was leather fringe hanging off of the vest and jeans and sequins and beads, too, but not too many that it was tacky. Just enough that it shimmered in the light.

Hazel set her costume aside lovingly and rummaged through the trunk.

"Here's my Miss America costume from three years ago, it'll fit you, but I dunno, it might be a little stupid,"

Hazel said as she tossed a long blonde wig, sequined dress, and white sash out of the trunk and in Lilac's general direction.

"Oh you might like this purple fairy one more, Lilac, I think this is more you..." Hazel added, throwing glittery purple wings and a giant tutu to Lilac. Lilac wasn't sure what to think. She did like purple. But a giant tutu? She might feel a little... conspicuous in something like that.

"What about Batman!" Finn called out. "That's one of my old costumes. I think Lilac would be an awesome... Bat Girl."

Lilac laughed. "I could be Bat Girl," she shrugged, and Hazel tossed her a black plastic mask and jumpsuit.

"OH MY GOD!" Hazel screamed from the trunk.

Lilac's heart began to thump, and panic seized up inside her.

"I FOUND CANDY FROM TWO YEARS AGO!" Hazel screamed at the top of her lungs. "BAGS OF IT!"

"What!" Finn said as he jumped up from the TV and ran to the trunk. "You're kidding me." He said when he looked inside. "Does Mom know about this?" he said in a whisper.

Hazel shook her head, slowly, no. Her eyes were wide and glittering.

"Do you think it's still... good?" Lilac asked.

"Well let's find out!" Finn said as he tore open a

package of candy corn.

Lilac and Hazel watched him intently, not sure what to expect. He chewed very carefully, his eyes narrowed. His chewing slowed.

"Well?" Hazel said.

"They're SO GOOD!" Finn laughed as he poured a giant handful and tossed them into his mouth. "Still tastes totally fresh. These are my favorite!"

"Gimme some!" Hazel said as she grabbed the bag and got a handful for herself. "Have some, Lilac," she said.

"Um... Does it taste like... corn?" Lilac asked hesitantly.

Hazel and Finn looked at each other, then burst out laughing.

"You've never had candy corn?!" Hazel got the words out through choking laughter and a mouth of candy. "Seriously?" She giggled.

Lilac shook her head, no.

"It doesn't taste like corn, just sugar!" Hazel said as she poured some into Lilac's hand.

Lilac tried one. Her eyes lit up. It was absolutely delicious. It did taste just like sugar. But soft, delicious, magnificent sugar. It was the best sugar she'd ever tasted in her entire life.

"Blaaah!" Finn had made fangs out of candy corn,

and was pretending to be a vampire.

"Chocolate, Juju Bees, Butterfingers... Candy Corn... Chuckles..." Hazel giggled as she called out of the candy they'd found in the trunk. "Oh, and my witch costume from two years ago! Lilac, what about this one? Here's the witch hat..." She said, reaching a hand back and giving Lilac a pointed black hat.

"Wow, thank you!" Lilac said. "A witch would be perfect!" The hat was kind of crumpled, but Lilac straightened it up, and it actually looked pretty good.

"And here's the robe and the striped stockings..." Hazel handed them to Lilac. She rummaged more.

"Finn, where's that green makeup?"

"I dunno, I used it for my monster face two years ago," Finn said.

Hazel took out a small plastic box that was smeared with different colors of makeup and bright red fake blood. "Here it is!" Hazel opened the box and handed Lilac a squished and mostly empty tube of green makeup. "That should be enough for your face."

"Oh, gimme that fake blood, Haze!" Finn called out when he saw the makeup box. She tossed it to him. "And a Butterfinger." he said. She ripped open the bag of Butterfingers and threw one to him. She tossed a Butterfinger at Lilac, who didn't quite catch it, and had to pick it up off of the floor.

"I'll try to come to Halloween with you," Lilac said, "I might even, um..." She added sheepishly, "I might even you know... sneak out."

"Yeah, Skully!" Finn said in excitement. "Don't let 'em hold you down! This is our night! It's our right as kids." He nodded.

"ALL kids go to Halloween," Hazel looked at her, eyes twitching and narrow. "It's a tradition!"

They settled in to watch cartoons, and Lilac sampled all of the different kinds of candy, none of which she'd ever had before, other than the plain chocolate.

About an hour later, there was a knock at the door and then the immediate sound of a woman's voice.

"Kids?" It was Patricia, Hazel and Finn's mom, followed by Sue Ann, who had returned for Lilac.

"You've GOT to let Lilac come with us to Halloween," Hazel jumped up and said to Sue instantly, although they had not yet met.

Sue laughed a little bit uncomfortably. "Oh, we'll see..." She hesitated.

Just by the way she was talking, Lilac could tell she probably wasn't going to be allowed. But she was fairly certain she was going to sneak out, anyway. Since the Mulligans were meeting with the Ghost Guard at six for a "long night," that would give Lilac plenty of time, she reckoned, especially if the entire Ghost Guard was captured. And she guessed they probably would be since they weren't letting her help or listening to the important things she had to say.

"I'd really like to go out for Halloween!" Lilac said. "I've got a costume that Hazel let me borrow and everything." Lilac motioned to the robe and stockings in her arms and put the hat on.

"Well, we'll have to talk about it, Lilac," Sue replied and motioned for Lilac to get up and leave. "I've exchanged numbers with Mrs. Cross," she said, "So let's discuss this when we get home, and then you can give them a call back, okay?"

Lilac agreed.

"Take the costume with you!" Hazel said. Lilac nodded and said her goodbyes, thanking them for the costume and everything. She hopped back into the front seat of the Mulligans' car and reached up to feel the brim of the witch hat. A rush of excitement washed over her.

She had a glorious costume. And whether or not she had permission, she was going to find a way to go to Halloween at the Seaside Fun Park.

5.
LILAC'S LUCK

"**B**ut I'll be in cos-tuuuume!" Lilac emphasized. "No one will even know who I am! I'll be unrecognizable and there will be hundreds of other kids in costume. It'll be impossible for Gremory to find me."

The Mulligans looked at each other.

"No more tonight, Lilac," Bobby Joe said. "Let's talk about it tomorrow."

"But tomorrow's Hallowee-eee-eee-eeen!" she tried to say without whining. But it was no use.

Even though she planned to sneak out anyway, it was the principle of the matter. The point that she'd be unrecognizable in costume was far more logical than the fear that she might be seen. There was no way Gremory's people would recognize her, not on Halloween, anyway.

She went back to the small spare room and lay on the bed with the lights off. It was late in the evening, and she was not tired at all. She heard the Mulligans shut off the TV just after ten. They went to their bedroom and closed the door, although Lilac could hear them talking in hushed voices.

Lilac crept silently down the hallway and stood outside their door, concentrating as hard as she could on what they were saying.

"She's got a point, Bobby," Sue said.

"We said we'd take responsibility for her," Bobby responded.

"Her father never said anything specific about her not going anywhere other than Skully Manor, which she's already been to. And we're going to be busy anyway, in the middle of an incredibly dangerous mission that both of us wish we hadn't gotten involved with in the first place," Sue sounded exasperated. "It might be good to give her something to do... you know, while we're gone. Keep her out of the way and out of trouble." Sue's strained whisper was getting louder. "Patty Cross said she could even stay the night at their house. And she might try to interfere with the mission and blow the whole thing if we don't give her something fun to do."

Lilac heard Bobby Joe sigh.

"You're probably right about that," he said.

Lilac silently opened her mouth in protest from the other side of the door. Is that what they thought? She was going to blow the whole thing, huh? Well, then, maybe she'd forgo the Fun Park after all, and show up at the roadhouse just to save the day. They'd likely get captured anyway since they weren't listening to her. Or maybe she'd sacrifice her first Halloween and sneak into the lab again to rescue her father. That's what she really wanted, anyway. And that was always an option, she figured. She'd got in there once before, although she'd barely gotten out. But she could still try again, now that she was wiser and more experienced.

"It *would* keep her out of the way tomorrow night," she heard Bobby say.

And with that, Lilac turned around and went back to the bedroom. She lay in the dark. She desperately wanted to go to Halloween with her friends, but now it sounded like they just wanted her out of the way. That's what Gremory had told her, too. And how many times had her father said that? It was all too familiar. No one listened to her. She frowned and pouted, but then her eyes narrowed, and her lower lip curled up.

There was one spirit who still might listen, if Lilac could just find her again. The Blue Lady.

Lilac waited 'till the Mulligans fell asleep. Then she put on her coat and boots and whispered quietly to Casper, who was curled up on the bed. "I'll be right back. Be very quiet. No meowing under any circumstances, okay?"

Lilac followed the same silent path as she had the night before, out of the Mulligans' house and across the outskirts of town on the scooter, towards the old cemetery and the roadhouse that sat silently a few blocks behind Skully Manor.

When she arrived, she tucked herself into the bushes.

She waited. Nothing happened. She waited longer. Still, nothing happened. She thought about going into the roadhouse, and then realized what a terrible idea that was, since it was filled with ghosts and spooks of all sorts—including Christopher Stefengraph and probably other henchmen from Gremory that she'd never recognize—but they might recognize her. Not to mention she'd been told to stay away multiple times.

Yet she stood up, left the scooter tucked in the bushes, and darted across the street. She ran for the roadhouse door. Just as she was about to open it, a bright light came out of nowhere. It was unnaturally bright—so bright—Lilac wasn't sure what was happening. She thought it might be aliens. Or maybe she had somehow just instantly died, and this was the end.

"Hey, you're the little girl from the old Skully place." A woman's voice said.

Lilac turned around and gasped, a terrible shuddering, inhaling gasp. Her face twisted into a mess of panic, shock, and pure terror. Her arms flailed up and clenched. If it had been a wild animal, Lilac Skully would have been dead meat. But it was not a wild animal.

It was Officer Grimble. The local police woman who patrolled Lilac's neighborhood, and who Lilac had met recently when the officer responded to one of Gremory's break-ins at Skully Manor.

When Lilac realized this, she took a bit of a breath.

"It's a little late to be out, isn't it?" the officer asked her.

"I was... looking for my cat?" Lilac said.

"Well, you'll just have to put some food out for him or... look in the morning," Officer Grimble replied.

"Hop in the car, I'll take you back home," she nodded her head towards the dark, rickety silhouette of Skully Manor, just a block or two away, the tallest structure in the area.

"Oh, I'll just ride my scooter back, my house is so close, and..." Lilac's heart was pounding. There were so many things going through her head right now, she had no idea how to process them. She just needed to get this insanely bright light off of her, get away from the roadhouse, and find some time to think.

"Scooter?" Grimble asked.

"In the bushes," Lilac said.

"Okay, then, let's get going now, I'll follow you in my

patrol car and make sure you get back alright."

"Oh th... thanks but..."

"No 'but's' about it!" Grimble laughed.

Lilac skirted across the street, with Officer Grimble's freakishly bright spotlight following her in a beam. It felt like the "beam of shame" to Lilac. She got on the scooter and scooted as fast as she could. Grimble's patrol car fired up and more lights came on. And the car began to follow her, lights blaring, scoot by scoot—down the road to Skully Manor.

Lilac tried to stay on the sidewalk and out of the light, but it was impossible. She felt like the entire world—at least the entire neighborhood—was watching. Probably even the ghosts from inside the manor. How utterly embarrassing.

When she got to the intersection just before her house, she froze. Her embarrassment turned to panic. There, idling at the corner, was one of the white vans from Gremory's lab. And there she was, the small, pale form illuminated in plain view from the lights on Officer Grimble's car.

She darted as fast as she could, across the street and through the back gate of Skully Manor. She heard the van's tires screech and take off through the intersection towards her house. And then she saw more flashing lights. And heard the wail of a siren. Then the sound of tires screeching again as Officer Grimble took off in pursuit of the van.

Lilac did not hang around. Blood raced through her as she jumped over the wall at the side of the garden, throwing the scooter with her. She dashed through the vacant lot on the other side of Skully Manor, in the darkest shadows she could find. She scooted through a small apartment courtyard with a little fountain. She said a prayer as she passed by the bubbling water and the statues of tiny plump birds. She maneuvered a few blocks away from her usual route, flying as fast as she could on the scooter.

Maybe Officer Grimble would catch the van and bust into the lab, and her father would be freed. She doubted it, but there was a chance. Not much of a chance. But a chance. Maybe. She could always go back to the police and tell them on her own. But... no. No. She'd be taken away from her father. They'd say he was crazy. Negligent. Just like before, when she was little. She didn't have anyone else but him. And she would consider it no more.

She raced down the darkest side street she could find, the scooter bumping up and down over tree roots that pushed up the sidewalk.

"I just wish I knew what to do," Lilac sighed. "I wish there was somewhere to go for advice in this kind of situation."

Something caught her eye up ahead. It was bright and purpley, and it blinked slowly, back and forth.

Psychic. Advice. Psychic. Advice. The words alternated in blinding neon letters.

"Madame Celestine" it said underneath in a cursive font with a crystal ball and a star. And then, "Open."

"Hmm... Well. Looks friendly enough. It can't hurt?" she whispered to herself, and she scooted across the street.

Lilac reached the door and surveyed the building. The glass front widows of the small shop were blacked out by a glossy film, and there was not another soul around as far as Lilac could tell—living or dead—for several blocks.

She hesitated with her hand on the door, and just as she was about to change her mind, the door pulled back away from her.

A rush of warm, fragrant air whooshed out with a soft glow of ambient rose light.

"Hello," a woman's voice said out from the light. "Can I help you, sweetie?"

"Oh, I..." Lilac stuttered. "I well, um..."

"Are you looking for something?" the woman asked again, still silhouetted so Lilac could not see the details of her face.

"Y... yes... exactly," Lilac said.

"Do you have cash?" The woman replied.

"Oh, well, um, a little?" Lilac said.

"Come in." The woman stepped to the side with a whoosh of sweet-smelling smoke, her hand, adorned with silver rings at all knuckles and stones of all colors, extended into the soft light.

Lilac hesitated for a moment, mouth agape. Then she pushed the scooter forward and into the perfumed air of the fortune teller's shop.

"Wow!" Lilac exclaimed. The shop was beautiful, like nothing she'd seen before. Purple and blue tapestries with depictions of ancient people and strange symbols, plants, stars, and creatures hung from all of the walls and the ceiling. There was a large round table in the center of the room, which was empty except for a purple-and-green crystal ball and a deck of cards. Four white pillars stood—one in each corner—each set with numerous candles, crystals, statutes, and other trinkets that looked as if they had great symbolism, but of what, Lilac was not sure.

The woman stood on one side of the round table and motioned to Lilac. Lilac could see her now in the dim light.

She was short, a bit round and curly haired with a pretty face, dressed all in draping black layers, and friendly enough—just enough—so Lilac wasn't frightened. The woman stared intently at Lilac through crooked wire-rimmed glasses, as if she was trying to place her from somewhere or look deep into her soul.

"An unexpected visit from a little girl with white hair," the woman said, breaking the silence and Lilac's wonder.

"My name is Celestine," the woman said and smiled. "Have a seat," she motioned and raised her eyebrows as if to ask Lilac's name.

"Oh, I'm Lilac," Lilac said, then regretted telling her.

The woman's eyebrows twitched, almost unintelligibly.

"Lilac," she repeated with a smile. "A spiritual flower, one that repels ghosts," she said. "Have you found that to be true?"

"Oh well, I...." Lilac didn't know how to answer. No, in short. Not at all. She had not found that to be true.

"Sit, sit," Celestine motioned.

Lilac sat.

"My usual price for a tarot reading is twenty dollars," she told Lilac.

"Oh, I," Lilac stammered.

"But tell me what you have, and what you want to know, Lilac, and we'll see what we can do." She smiled, trustingly.

Lilac took out the money in her pocket. Eight dollars in bills and some change. She put the five dollar bill on the table.

Celestine nodded, then got up from her chair to retrieve a small black cauldron and a bundle of leaves. The fortune teller lit a match, then set the leaves on fire inside the cauldron. A cloud of white smoke billowed out. It smelled pleasantly sweet but also herbal and bitter.

Celestine sat back down and crossed her hands.

"Now," she said to Lilac seriously, "what do you want to know?"

Lilac stared back, "Um, well, I…. I want to know how to rescue my father." She nodded. "Please," she added as politely as she could.

"Oh," Celestine's face drew serious. "Well, the cards may not be able to tell you exactly that. They speak in generalities, but they can give you clues."

She picked up the cards and shuffled them well. "Let's see." She closed her eyes as she shuffled the cards more. "Lilac wants to know how to rescue her father," she repeated.

"Um…" Lilac asked shyly, eyeing the large and gorgeous purple-and-green swirling crystal ball. "I was hoping to use the crystal ball," she said, "Like the one on the sign out front?" she smiled sweetly.

Celestine laughed. "Tell you what, you come back another night, with the full twenty dollars, and I'll give you a deal on that ritual. But tonight, I can do tarot cards. I've got a friend coming in a few minutes."

Lilac shrugged. "Okay." She said.

Celestine took the five dollar bill off of the table and slipped it in her skirt pocket. "Now." She shuffled the cards well for a few moments, repeated what Lilac wanted to know, then placed the deck in front of Lilac. "With your left hand, cut the deck." She said.

"Just... just pick up half of it?" Lilac asked.

Celestine nodded.

"Do I look at them?" Lilac clarified.

"No." Celestine replied.

Lilac picked up some of the cards and set them aside.

Celestine turned over the first three cards from the original pile, rapidly. Her lower lip curled down and her eyebrows up, then she looked at Lilac as if she were surprised, possibly impressed. "Oh," she said.

Lilac's interest perked up, and she looked at the cards.

"The Emperor. The Five of Cups. The Empress," Celestine explained and then looked at Lilac again with woeful eyes. The fortune teller thought long and hard before she pulled two more cards. Her eyes widened, and then she smiled. "Three of Cups. Ten of Cups."

She then lay the first three cards in front of Lilac.

Lilac looked at them.

The first card showed a man on a throne, like a king. The second card depicted the most sorrowful cloaked figure that Lilac could have imagined. And the third card had a picture of a beautiful woman sitting on a throne.

"The loss of your mother has caused your father great sorrow. The Emperor. The Five of Cups, The Empress." She repeated again as she pointed to each card in order.

Lilac stuttered, and her breath stopped for a moment.

"The first card you drew is the representation of your father. That's not a coincidence, Lilac. You came here and asked about your father, hmm?" She gave Lilac a serious look.

Lilac nodded once.

"And now, you're lost in the middle of it." The woman said. "And to *find* your father..." She pointed to the next two cards. "What do you see in this card, Lilac?"

Lilac looked at the card. There were three robed women dancing together and holding up golden goblets. They looked happy.

"Friends?" Lilac asked.

"Friendship. The Three of Cups." Celestine nodded as she pointed to the card. "Connection through emotion." Then she pointed to the last card, the Ten of

Cups. "What do you see in this card, Lilac?"

Lilac looked at the card. It had a rainbow going over a clear blue sky, with ten golden cups shining through. There was a man and a woman each holding one arm around the other and their other hand up into the air, with children playing nearby. A lump formed in Lilac's throat, and she felt as if she couldn't speak.

"What do you see, Lilac?" Celestine said again.

"H... happiness?" Lilac choked out the word before she burst into tears. "And family." She said with a terrible sob.

"Yes." Celestine said. "You've suffered a life of loss and loneliness, Lilac. More than most. But you will find your family, your happiness, and your father. And your friends will help you. They will get you there, if you trust them."

Lilac sobbed even harder. "I don't have any friends that can help with this and... " She gasped. "But... maybe the Blue Lady's my friend!" Lilac looked up with wide eyes of realization. "And she wears a robe, just like on this card! Except it's blue!" She pointed to the card. "Oh my god!" Lilac exclaimed. "I gotta find her! Do you know where I can find the Blue Lady? Or the Ghost Guard?"

"No." Celestine replied abruptly. "I don't know anything about that. And if you want another reading, it's another five dollars."

Lilac scrunched up her nose and her mouth to one side. Celestine handed her a tissue, and she blew her nose.

Suddenly the door swung open behind them. Lilac turned around startled as she saw the outline of a squat, hooded figure.

"Cerridwen!" Lilac exclaimed as she jumped up from the chair and ran towards the old witch.

"Well," Cerridwen said as her eyes adjusted to the light and she got a look at Lilac. "If it isn't the little witch," she said, pinching Lilac's cheek just a bit. Lilac beamed.

"Do you know where I can find the Blue Lady or the Ghost Guard? I've gotta rescue my father and... she's the only one who... and... it looked like her on one of the cards!" Lilac pointed to the cards on the table with excitement.

Celestine cut in. "I see you two know each other." She exchanged a smile with Cerridwen. "Lilac came in to get some information."

"Well, I hope you got what you are looking for." Cerridwen winked at Lilac, through a deeply wrinkled eye.

"Um... yes, but I still need to know where Blue is or the Ghost Guard's headquarters. I think I might need to ask another question, but I don't have another five dollars," Lilac admitted.

The two women burst into laughter and then looked kindly at Lilac. Cerridwen set her hand on Lilac's shoulder.

"Well," she smiled, "sometimes you just need to let it sink in." She nodded.

Lilac supposed, but that didn't make her feel much better. She'd come here for answers. And she still didn't have quite what she needed.

"And," Cerridwen added as her eyes twinkled. "I've heard that the library—not the one downtown, but the one on the outskirts by the covered bridge..." She paused for emphasis and nodded slowly. "The one in the old church with the tall white steeple." She said very carefully. "*That* library is haunted." She winked again. "Or so I've heard."

Lilac beamed. "Okay!" She said. "Thank you!" She jumped forward and hugged Cerridwen, who hugged her back with a warm embrace that smelled like cinnamon, cloves, and dirt from a freshly dug garden.

"Take this," Celestine said as she took a small pale blue stone out of her pocket and handed it to Lilac. "It'll bring the protection of your guardian angels, so you won't be so alone on your journey."

Lilac's eyes brightened as she gazed at the stone. "Thank you!" she said to Celestine, then tucked the stone into her pocket.

Celestine motioned towards the door. "Well, it was lovely to meet you tonight, Lilac. Winny and I have some business to attend to, so I'll have to..."

"Oh no problem!" Lilac said. "I'll go now.... um... Thank you! Nice to meet you too. I hope I see you both again!"

"I have no doubt you will." Cerridwen smiled with her terribly wrinkly eyes and patted Lilac's cheek.

Celestine welcomed Lilac to come back anytime for a reading at a discount, and she led Lilac to the door.

Lilac picked up her scooter and shuffled into the night.

As she scooted off, the vision of the cards and what Celestine and Cerridwen said floated through her mind.

It was all terribly true, what she'd seen in the cards. Her family had been ripped apart by grief and sadness, and the loss of her mother had caused her father great sorrow. And those were the cards that Lilac had pulled. Father. Sorrow. Mother. And the other two cards. Friendship. Happiness and family. And the women in robes, just like Blue. She got chills as she scooted along, the tires crunching over gigantic dried maple leaves scattered over the sidewalks.

As she approached the library, she recognized it instantly. It was the one she'd been to a few times after begging her father to let her go, the one where she'd checked out books that were now overdue and still hiding under the floorboards in the kitchen. She felt a sweeping pang of guilt. The library was in an old church, and it made her feel even more guilty as she got closer.

The library was shadowed by massive oak trees, the branches reaching out and over like a skeleton's hand. It looked dark. Yet, as she rounded the corner, she caught a faint glimpse of a glimmer in the back basement window. It was the slightest glowing tinge of bluish green.

The glint of a ghost.

Lilac jumped off of the scooter and dashed forward. She crouched down and cupped her hands to look down through the low window. There was an entire meeting of ghosts! She almost couldn't believe it. She surveyed the crowd of ten or twelve spirits, and recognized Luther's glittering black figure. And a few seats away from him, Blue! Her heart leapt in joy, and she smiled. She'd done it! It was the Ghost Guard! She found them!

An apparition appeared suddenly on the other side of the glass. It was a woman that Lilac did not recognize. Her keen eyes, amplified hugely in size by thick glasses attached to a beaded chain, gazed at Lilac in a silent, scolding manner. Her hair was pulled back tightly in a bun. She had her arms crossed in front of her, holding a couple of books, and she wore a name tag on her brown tweed high-collared dress, with a ghostly script that read, "Minerva—Head Librarian."

Lilac saw Minerva pointing her out in the window to the room full of ghosts.

Her stomach sank. She swallowed and took a deep breath. This was it. This was her big chance. Lilac waved through the window to Blue and the rest of the ghosts, then got up, and ran to the basement door.

It opened with a cold, swift swoosh.

Lilac stopped in the doorway. The circle of ghosts had all turned to look at her. There were a range of faces, some young, some old. Some looked kind like Blue, and some looked terribly menacing, like Luther. Some looked bemused, curious, or skeptical. But they were all focused on her, intently, their dark eyes swirling, watching, and waiting.

The scent of ancient leather library books and a bit of mold wafted out around her. The room ahead was dark and shadowy—illuminated only by the light of the moon and the flickering, faint spectral glow of the Ghost Guard.

She took a step forward, then froze. With the last amount of courage she had, she took two more small steps, and the door closed behind her as swiftly as it as opened.

A tremble ran through her, and she knew that if she didn't say something now, she never would. So, she spoke.

"I'm Lilac Skully," She said to the room, as a chill hit—so dense, so freakishly goosebump-inducing that she almost fell to her knees. "And I'm here..." she said as her voice wavered, "to give you some very important information."

None of the ghosts spoke. Blue looked at her, her face unmoving. Luther glared. Minerva pursed her lips in disapproval. Lilac wondered if Minerva knew she had overdue books checked out, and if she was going to be in trouble or have to pay some sort of a huge fine. She only had about three dollars left.

Lilac's attention fell to the spirit of a woman who might've been over a hundred years old, hunched over so incredibly far that her back was like a ball. Her hands grasped a well-worn wooden staff with a crystal on top, glowing ever so slightly pinkish. Her face was encouraging, beckoning, and waiting for Lilac to continue.

"Y... you guys are walking into a trap. The people from Gremory found out about your plans and... well they're actually capturing ghosts at the Seaside Fun Park on Halloween, not the roadhouse!" Lilac said, as calmly and logically as she could.

Luther clutched his head and groaned, bending forward dramatically as if it was the most absurd thing he'd ever heard. "Where are the living handlers for this kid? Are they doing anything to contain her?"

Some of the ghosts began to grumble and chatter amongst themselves.

"Perhaps!" A weak voice called out, as loudly as it could, and everyone stopped. "Maybe we should listen. A little bit more." It was the old woman with the staff.

"Where did you hear this?" she asked Lilac.

"From the ghosts in my house. Milly and Archie said the men from Gremory broke in to Skully Manor again and they heard them talking…"

The chatter around the room broke out once more.

"Are you talking about those two brats in the old manor house?" Luther's loud voice broke out over the crowd. "Mere toddlers." He chuckled. "What would they know?"

Lilac saw Blue roll her eyes at him, but Blue did not speak up.

"Those are my friends," Lilac tried to explain. "And, they heard the men from Gremory talking about it! It's a trap for you guys, and…"

"Oh criminy." Luther stood up and began to pace behind his chair. "This is absolutely ridiculous."

"Lilac, please," Blue finally spoke. "We will discuss this and look into this. But you've got to trust us, and you're not to get involved any further."

A flush crept across Lilac's cheeks. She began to sweat under her coat. She had felt so sure. But did she really know what she was talking about? Milly and Archie had heard the men talking about it and... they must've heard correctly, right? Or... maybe not?

"Well," Lilac stammered, "I'm the one that rescued you... if you remember correctly. I... I...I..."

Blue looked at her sternly, and Lilac began to shake. Lilac had freed Blue, yes. But then Lilac had been captured. And she'd needed Blue to rescue her that night, too.

"Go back to the Mulligans', Lilac, and do not leave again until I come to you myself. Do you understand?" Blue whispered to her from across the room, so quietly, yet the entire Ghost Guard heard it, maybe the entire universe, because everything else was so deadly silent— you could hear a pin drop.

Lilac didn't know what else to do. Her face burned with embarrassment and despair. She turned around and pushed through the door before the ghosts could open it for her. She got back onto her scooter, and with a crushed spirit and a wobbly scoot, went back to the Mulligans' house.

6.
Bobbing for Bad Apples

ilac lay in bed for quite a while after the sun woke her up. She was miserable, for two reasons. Well, three, actually. The first was the mortifying events of last night. She thought for a moment there that she'd really be able to join the Ghost Guard. It had literally been her one chance to convince them. But she blew it. She blew it! Plus Luther's humiliating reaction to the whole thing, which she tried to erase from her memory, but hadn't succeeded yet. And what she'd said to Blue. And how she'd been scolded. What a total disaster.

The second thing making her miserable was Halloween. Surely the Mulligans weren't going to let her go to now. The Ghost Guard would tell them all about last night. And they'd probably lock her up and take her costume so she couldn't sneak out either. She'd ruined everything.

The third reason Lilac felt terribly awful this morning was because she smelled food. It smelled delicious, and she was starving. Yet she was so ashamed, she pretended she didn't need the Mulligans or their delicious food. For a while, anyway, until she could stand it no longer.

"Hi Lilac," Sue Ann said, as friendly as ever, when Lilac entered the kitchen.

"Hi," Lilac said back groggily, a half step away from retreating back to the spare room.

"We've decided," Sue Ann said to her, handing her a giant glass of orange juice and a plate of food that looked like some eggs in a half-moon shape, "that you can go out with Hazel and Finn for Halloween."

Lilac almost choked on her own spit. Her eyes lit up. "R... Really?" she said.

"Yes, Lilac, even after you snuck out last night. Again." Bobby Joe sighed.

"You... you found out... about last night...," Lilac said sheepishly. She wanted to ask how much they knew, but she didn't want to have to go through the horror of replaying any of the gruesome details, so she didn't ask.

They looked embarrassed for her and maybe for themselves, too.

"Well... I can really go? To trick or treat and to the Fun Park with Hazel and Finn?" she clarified.

"Yes," Sue nodded kindly, and Bobby Joe tried to smile too, but he rolled his eyes a little.

"I'm kind of jealous, actually," he chuckled to Sue.

Sue let out a heavy sigh.

"Thanks!" Lilac said, as her thoughts began to swirl, and the shame from last night at the library faded just a notch. "I won't get into any trouble, I swear!" she added.

"We're going to be out tonight on a Ghost Guard mission anyway," Sue tried to explain, "And we don't want you to worry about it. So this will give you something to do and keep your mind off of it while we're gone. And you'll be spending the night at Hazel and Finn's house."

Lilac thought she might explode, but she nodded quietly and began to eat. Halloween at the Fun Park. And spending the night with Hazel and Finn. It was a Halloween miracle. The food turned out to be an omelet with cheese. She'd never had an omelet before because the word sounded kind of gross. Fancy, but gross. But it was delicious. And the way Sue said she could go to Halloween was actually nice, and not at all like Lilac was being kept out of the way, even though she knew she kind of was.

The rest of the day dragged by. Lilac counted the minutes till she'd be dropped off with Hazel and Finn at five o'clock. She set her costume out on the bed hours earlier and tried to keep herself busy. She sifted through some books that Sue Ann had, but nothing really kept her attention. She watched some TV just to see the Halloween commercial come on, using it to try and kickstart daydreams about what lay ahead for her first night ever of trick-or-treating.

She took some notes and transferred some of the facts about the ghosts at the Fun Park from her mom's diary onto a loose sheet of paper. She folded the paper and tucked it in her pocket, along with the few dollars and coins that she had left, her lucky amulet, and the new crystal that Celestine had given her.

At three-thirty in the afternoon, she could no longer wait. The anticipation was burning inside of her. She put on her coat and the striped stockings from the costume— even though her own socks were also striped—then put the witch's robes over it all. She put on her black lace-up boots. She went into the bathroom with the green tube of makeup. She brushed and re-braided her hair, then squirted out a glob of gloopy pea green makeup and smeared it on her face. She took her time to make it look even all over, and put on the witch hat. She stood back. She looked at herself in the mirror, and narrowed her eyes.

Her face couldn't contain a bright smile. She loved

the way she looked. And she certainly didn't look like Lilac Skully anymore. She was just a little green witch, getting ready to fly out on Halloween night.

"Happy Halloween, Lilac." She whispered to herself in the mirror.

She still had over an hour till she was going to Hazel and Finn's. She made sure Casper had a big bowl of food because she was going to be staying the night with the Cross family. She sat and watched TV in her costume. She stared at the clock, and the minutes ticked by.

At 4:45 she knocked on the door of the garage where Sue and Bobby had been frantically busy with something all day.

"Come in!" Sue called to her.

Lilac opened the door. She was taken aback. It wasn't just because the energy in the room was intense. Lilac had assumed their garage would be more like Hazel and Finn's garage, filled with regular stuff, but apparently, this garage was the headquarters of the Mulligans' amateur paranormal research operation. And it didn't look as amateur as Lilac had expected. There was equipment stacked on all of the surfaces, much like Lilac's father's lab. There were antennas and wires and lights and town maps pinned to the walls with tacks.

"Are you ready to go?" Sue Ann seemed flustered

and distracted, downright nervous.

Bobby Joe was sweating. He had large headphones over his ears and did not look up to acknowledge Lilac. Neither of them said anything about her fantastic witch costume.

Lilac nodded politely to Sue Ann. She had the purple kitten pajamas under her arm, ready to spend the night.

Sue grabbed her keys and led Lilac unceremoniously to the car.

They drove to her friends' house in silence. Sue Ann was obviously preoccupied and Lilac was, too. She felt nervous butterflies in her stomach. Outside, groups of kids were trick-or-treating already with loads of candy and costumes of all sorts. Big, bright jack-o-lanterns lined the pathways and porches, and spooky decorations hung from the trees. Lilac rolled down the window a little and could hear the sound of laughter and silly haunted sound effects. She smelled the crisp autumn air, with maybe a chance of rain on the way. She saw several other children dressed as witches, which made her feel even more confident in her theory that she'd blend right in.

When they reached Hazel and Finn's house, Sue Ann didn't park or get out of the car. She left the engine running. Lilac's heart was thumping so loudly, she thought it might burst out of her chest.

"We'll be back for you in the morning," Sue Ann told Lilac. "Nine or ten."

Lilac nodded.

"Wish me luck, okay." Sue said, nervously.

And although Lilac thought Sue Ann sounded terribly unsure, Lilac, the little green witch, nodded three or four times intently, wished her good luck, thanked her, and hopped out of the car. She ran down the driveway to Hazel and Finn's clubhouse, clutching the witch hat to her head as Sue drove off.

Hazel and Finn were already eating candy. Their mother was going to stay home and answer the door for trick-or-treaters before her night shift at the hospital, but the kids had already taken quite a large stash of this year's candy for themselves.

"Have a Red Rope, Lilac!" Finn threw a long, red piece of candy at her from across the room. She caught it.

"You look good in that," Hazel said to her, admiring the costume she'd lent to Lilac.

"Your costume is amazing," Lilac said to Hazel. It was true. Hazel's greenish eyes and golden brown hair were shining out from under the pink-and-purple cowgirl hat.

"Thanks!" Hazel said, stuffing a piece of green gum into her mouth. "You want some gum?" She offered a package of gumballs to Lilac. Lilac nodded her head. It was a small cellophane package that had three gumballs inside, one red, one orange, and one yellow. Lilac knew the red one tasted like cherry, and her mouth was watering just looking at it.

"Let's go trick-or-treating!" Finn said, heading towards the door. "I'm gonna die if I can't go right now,"

"Lilac, where's your sack?" Hazel asked her. Lilac didn't have one. Hazel ran into the house and grabbed an old pillow sack.

"Let's go!" They motioned to her. Finn pulled the monster mask over his face. "We're leaving, Mom!" He shouted to his mother in the house.

"Okay! Have fun, kids!" Lilac heard from the house.

The three children ran down the driveway, the excitement racing in their blood, out into the fading light of Halloween night.

Lilac wasn't quite sure what to expect. She followed Hazel and Finn to the very next house. There was a simple jack-o-lantern on the stoop, with triangle eyes and a jagged mouth.

"TRICK OR TREAT!" Hazel and Finn screamed in unison as soon as the door opened.

Lilac jumped back, a bit bewildered and unsure of what to do next, and stood, mouth agape, saying nothing. The person at the door wasn't in a costume, but they pulled out a large bowl of candy and plunked one in each of Hazel and Finn's pillow sacks. Lilac held out her bag too, and candy was thrown in. She followed her friends to the next house.

"TRICK OR TREAT!" They yelled. This time, Lilac said it with them, slightly out of synch and not very loud, but she gave it a try. They got more candy, this time from a man wearing a bloody hatchet through his head. Lilac hoped it was fake. She thought it must be. They went to the next house.

"TRICK OR TREAT!" Lilac yelled at the top of her lungs. It felt incredible. A woman in a beautiful unicorn mask and wings gave them all chocolate.

The next house had two scarecrows out in front. They had pumpkins for heads and were both wearing spooky old-fashioned dresses.

"TRICK OR TREAT!" The three of them screamed when the door of the house opened. Lilac laughed and giggled, wide-eyed as she saw her favorite candy— orange fruit slices—go into her bag. They went to the next house. And the next. And the next.

There were jack-o-lanterns of all sorts, spooky faces, lights, and decorative ghosts made of paper and string. Lilac's bag was getting heavy. Her cheeks and stomach were beginning to feel sore from laughing and smiling.

She'd never had this much candy in her possession before, ever. Within fifteen or twenty minutes, all three children were giddy and running with delight from house to house.

When they approached a particularly stately home, Hazel slowed, and her face grew serious.

The front porch had tall white columns decorated with orange and black paper chains, streamers, gigantic fake spiders, and white ribbons done up to look like spider webs. There were huge bunches of helium balloons in black and orange on either side of the door.

"We don't have to go, Haze," Finn said to her, tapping her arm, "Let's just skip it,"

"No," Hazel said, taking a deep breath and raising her chin up a bit. "Let's go. Besides, I bet they have the best candy." She strode forward up the stone walkway, leading Finn and Lilac. She pressed the doorbell.

Bing-Bong, Bing-BONG went the particularly ostentatious doorbell.

"TRICK OR TREAT!" they all yelled when the door opened.

"Oh, oh! Well, hello there," said a woman in a beautiful red dress with a fancy hat and mask that only covered half of her face. She had a look of recognition when she saw Hazel and Finn. "Well, I wasn't expecting... I'm glad to see Jessica invited you...Why don't you come in..." the woman said.

Lilac saw Hazel shoot Finn a brief and mischievous glance.

Lilac followed through the entry into a large room. And she got a funny, sinking feeling as soon as she walked into the house. She tried to squelch it. The house was filled with children having a lively Halloween party. She had actually never been to a party before, so she didn't know if that was what was making her feel so strange, or if it was something else.

There were a dozen or more kids in costumes—mummies wrapped in strips of white linen, faces with elaborate monster makeup, and kids wearing fairy wings, witch hats, and plastic masks. The furniture had been pushed to the sides of the room, and a table was set up with bowls of chips, snacks, and plates of cupcakes with orange and brown frosting, cookies with sprinkles, and a big tub of bottled soda on ice.

The woman who had answered the door came in with another tray of hot food. It looked like mini-hamburgers to Lilac, and several of the children ran over to grab them. Then a tall, large-framed man carrying an aluminum tub broke through the crowd of children. He wore a simple costume, a black suit, a short black top hat, and a white mask that covered his eyes. Lilac stared at him, and she felt her skin crawl. There was something about him. What was it?

Hazel and Finn walked up to a girl in the center of the room. The girl was wearing a gigantic pale pink skirt and dress covered in sequins and a massive sparkly crown. She held up a glittery wand.

"Hi Jessica," Hazel and Finn said in unison, somewhat flat.

Jessica seemed taken slightly off-guard, but she was not shaken. She bopped her wand at them. "Who invited YOU?" She rolled her eyes in her mother's direction. "I guess my mom let you in." She sighed. "Well, okay, we're just about to bob for apples, anyway, I'm going first." She eyed Lilac up and down.

"Who are you?" Jessica said to Lilac, without waiting for an answer. "You don't go to my school. And what kind of witch are you supposed to be? I'm Glinda the Good Witch," Jessica told her, waving her wand around her gigantic puffy skirt.

"I'm Cerridwen, the bad witch," Lilac told Jessica with a straight face and without hesitating. She had almost said her name was Lilac, but she was glad she didn't. No one needed to know who she was.

The man in the white mask set the aluminum tub of water and apples in the center of the room, and then retreated to the doorway to watch with Jessica's mother.

Lilac's eyes followed him. She guessed it was Jessica's

father. She would have kept her eyes on him, but the kids began "bobbing for apples," a game which Lilac thought looked absolutely dreadful, like something she would never want to participate in—ever—so she watched it intently from a corner, her eyes wide in horror.

"Bobbing for apples" seemed to involved grabbing an apple out of the tub of water with your teeth, without using your arms. As you did this, water splashed everywhere, and the other kids heckled and taunted you, adding to the stress and intensity. Lilac slid around the edge of the room to the snacks and stood between the wall and the table in a small nook, several layers of children away from the apple bobbing and close by to Hazel and Finn, who were filling small orange plates with cupcakes and cookies.

Lilac took a cupcake. She took a bite. It was amazing. There were actual sprinkles on it, both chocolate and orange in color. She finished the cupcake and bit into a cookie with orange frosting. Her mouth watered, and she felt like she might just blast off into outer space. She hadn't eaten a sugar cookie since her father had brought home an old tin of small, rock hard cookies after Christmas several years ago.

She had enjoyed those cookies, but these had sprinkles and frosting on them, and they were soft. She was fairly certain they had been home-baked by the pretty mother in the red dress, most likely with love and care while she sang songs and let Jessica eat raw dough. It was the sweetest, most buttery thing she could have ever imagined.

"Good idea showing up at Jessica Black's house," Finn chuckled to Hazel, stuffing his mouth with a frosted cupcake. "Even if it is kind of awkward. I shoulda known the rich kid's neighborhood would have the best Halloween treats and parties."

Hazel nodded in agreement and took two cookies with her free hand.

Lilac froze, her mouth full of buttery sugar cookie. Black. She thought. Jessica Black. Her brain ran at high speed. Black. Black. Black. Black. Black. And Gremory. She looked over at Jessica's father. Could it be? No. Black must be a common name. Of course it was. Very common. Jessica's father was leaning against the arched doorway, watching the children play with his wife by his side. The white mask over his eyes made it hard for her to see his face. But there was something about it, something Lilac could still not discern. She got cold chills and leaned against the back wall of the room, clutching two cookies, one orange and one with black-and-white frosting done up to look like a spider web, topped with a plastic spider.

Lilac watched Finn bob for apples while she ate the

spider cookie in the corner, placing the plastic spider in her pocket and keeping a close eye on Jessica's father. Then she watched Finn convince Hazel to bob for apples. He held her pink-and-purple cowgirl hat while she adeptly bobbed and got an apple pretty much on her first try, then rolled her eyes at Jessica, who had not been able to get an apple at all with the gigantic crown pinned to her head.

"Come on, Skully! You next!" Finn's boisterous voice rung out over the crowd.

"Yeah come on, Lilac!" Hazel shouted and ran towards her.

Lilac froze. She did not want to bob for apples, not at all. But there was something else. Someone was watching her now. Her eyes darted to Jessica Black's father. He was looking right at her. His dark eyes shone with disbelief from underneath the white mask.

Lilac ran. She did not hesitate. She bolted through the crowd of children and out the front door of the house. She didn't look back to see if anyone was following her.

"Lilac!" she heard Hazel's voice running up behind her. She didn't stop.

"Lilac!" she heard Finn yell, this time closer as he caught up to her.

"I..." Lilac had no idea how to explain this one. She couldn't, could she? That she was fairly certain Jessica

Black's father was a terrible man who had kidnapped a substantial number of ghosts as well as her own father? "I don't want to bob for apples!" Lilac finally blurted out, hoping that would suffice as an excuse.

"Okay, no big deal," Hazel said, "Don't freak out, Skully."

Lilac shushed her and looked around for anyone that might have heard.

"Is someone... looking for you, Lilac?" Hazel was starting to sense something was amiss.

"That party was lame anyway other than the food," Finn said quickly.

Lilac wasn't sure if he was changing the subject on purpose or not, but she was grateful either way.

"Let's go to the Seaside Fun Park!" Finn blurted out and took off running.

Hazel and Lilac followed without question. Lilac did her best to keep up, but after what seemed like a mile or more, she started to lose steam. She was not as sporty as Hazel and Finn.

"Wait up!" She called to them, and they slowed to a walk. Finn used the opportunity to eat a chocolate bar out of his trick-or-treat bag.

"How much farther is it?" Lilac panted.

"What?!" Hazel yelled. "You've never been there before?!" She added in disbelief.

"I've always wanted to," Lilac said back politely with wide eyes. She had. The Seaside Fun Park was a place of local legend, and even if you didn't like the scarier rides, the sun and the beach and the food and festive atmosphere looked and felt irresistible to kids. Even to indoorsy kids like Lilac Skully.

"We're almost there," Finn said.

They trotted forward and approached a stop light at a larger intersection.

Hazel and Finn jumped up and down excitedly. It seemed like they could not wait one more moment for the light to change to green.

The light changed and the children ran across, illuminated by the bright street lights in the intersection. Lilac followed a few steps behind. They crossed the street, and Hazel and Finn kept running. They approached a dimly lit block where the street lights had ended. Lilac was losing ground, falling farther behind.

"Wait, guys!" she called out, her quiet voice not quite cutting through as she tried to hurry her step.

Then Lilac heard the screech of tires behind her and the roar of an engine. She looked back. It was a white van with dark tinted windows. She gasped and screamed. Hazel and Finn heard her and turned around. The van swerved towards Lilac, its wheels jumping up over the sidewalk. The man in the driver's seat opened his door, his arm reaching out to grab her. A top hat. A white mask.

Lilac fell back and rolled the other way, feeling the wind of the speeding van rush past her, swooping in much too close. The van screeched and swerved, nearly hitting Hazel and Finn as it tried to regain its traction. Hazel and Finn screamed, Finn held his arms out protectively, yet uselessly, to shield his sister. The van narrowly missed them and sped off down the street in a roar. Hazel and Finn ran to Lilac and helped pick her up. Her candy had been thrown out of the bag all over the ground, and they collected as much as they could.

"Let's get out of here!" Lilac said to them, still shaking.

They didn't hesitate.

7.
HALLOWEEN
AT THE SEASIDE FUN PARK

"Are you guys okay?" Finn asked the girls as they had retreated to the shadows of a different street.

"Yeah," Hazel said.

"Yeah," Lilac said, although her heart felt like it was going to pound out of her chest, and she wasn't done shaking yet.

"Who was that?" Hazel asked.

"I dunno," Lilac said.

"I hate kidnappers!" Finn said. "What is wrong with some grown-ups?" He shook his head. "Why can't they just leave us kids alone?!"

"Do you want to go home, Lilac?" Hazel asked.

"No," Lilac replied. "There's no way I'm missing this."

They continued at a trot, darting back and forth

106

through the dark shadows of the streets.

"We're almost there!" Finn yelled. They ran through the courtyard of an apartment complex, through a little garden with a thick hedge.

"Stash your candy bags under here," he whispered. "We don't wanna be carrying them around the park, I swear they'll still be here when we get back," he said, and Lilac and Hazel tucked their sacks away.

They ran till they came out onto a seaside bluff.

Lilac gasped as she took in the sweeping ocean view. A wharf and the Seaside Fun Park were just a ways down the coast, with a huge white-and-red roller coaster and a Ferris wheel lit up in blue, orange, and green. Delighted screams of people on the rides hung in the air.

"Oh! Look at the moon!" Hazel exclaimed.

Lilac and Finn were speechless when they spotted it. It was huge—hanging low and golden over the ocean, lighting up the entire coastline with an ethereal glow.

Throngs of people in all sorts of costumes were walking in the same direction, all hurrying down to the Seaside Fun Park. The three children blended into a large group of kids and continued down and around a curve in the road 'till more of the coastline was revealed.

"The lighthouse!" Lilac exclaimed when she saw it.

"Yeah it's not as cool anymore," Finn said, "It used to be fun, but now they never light the big fire thing inside it, so what's the point?"

Lilac pretended to agree, but her mind raced with what she'd read about the lighthouse in her mother's diary. That's where her parents had been involved in a big paranormal research project! Her heart skipped a beat, and she tried to hop up a bit to get a better view of it.

"Wait till you see the fireworks at midnight, though!" Finn said. "They're amazing, and in all the Halloween colors like orange and purple and green."

"It's so cool, Lilac!" Hazel shouted. "The best fireworks, ever."

Lilac had never seen any fireworks in person before, so she couldn't imagine how wonderful it must be. She couldn't wait to see it.

"Boom!" Finn said. "They use gunpowder and shoot glitter up into the sky!"

They approached the entrance, a magnificent red-and-white-striped tent with a banner. It said "Halloween Carnival" in lettering she recognized from the commercial. There was a gang of clowns with pumpkin heads. They wore black-and-white-striped suits, massive mis-matched green and purple shoes, and they were taunting all the people passing by.

"It's the skeleton from the commercial!" Lilac said with wonder when she saw someone dressed up just like him, welcoming everyone to the park. She took a deep breath to calm herself and ran to keep up with her friends.

She followed them through a door and into the arcade. Her eyes darted this way and that, trying to take in the magnificent lights and colors as they bounced off the walls. The roar of pinball, games, shouts, bells, and music filled her ears. The arcade was packed with hundreds of children in costumes—more children than Lilac had ever seen in her entire life—and she struggled to keep up with Hazel and Finn amidst the pandemonium and revelry.

They passed a brightly lit stand selling candy apples. Lilac had never seen candy apples in person, but there they were. They looked like pure magic, better than she'd imagined. Some were dipped in caramel and then in nuts. Some were covered with chocolate or white chocolate and decorated with rainbow sprinkles, crunched up pretzels, or chocolate chips. She would have stopped to stare at the bins of colorful candy shaped like fruits, the massive chunks of fudge with marshmallows, and endless flavors of saltwater taffy, but Lilac trotted off quickly so as not to lose her friends.

Hazel and Finn ran to the ticket booth. It was painted in garish pink and orange stripes with an overhang of tattered blue fabric.

"Three, please!" Finn said to the window, and Hazel pulled a wad of bills out of her pocket.

Lilac hesitated, she didn't have enough money.

"Mom gave us extra for you," Hazel said.

Lilac said thanks very quietly, then hoped they had heard her. She watched Hazel and Finn stick their arms through the small hole in the window, and two hands put neon green papery bracelets around their wrists.

Lilac did the same thing and tried to stay cool. But she could barely contain a huge smile on her face. She looked down at the wristband once it was taped around her wrist. "Halloween Carnival at the Seaside Fun Park," the bracelet said. It was bright green with black and white print. It had a small picture of the skeleton's face from the commercial and an outline of the roller coaster. Lilac thought she would never take it off, if it lasted, for as long as she ever lived. And then when it did fall off, she'd cherish the remnants of it forever.

She tried not to squeal. Or explode. But she had to jump up and down to release some of the overwhelming grandiosity of it all. It was as if all the lonely moments of her life that had led up to this night had vanished. Poof. She felt like Cinderella. This was really happening. She was out with friends on Halloween.

"Come on!" Finn called to her, and the twins took off again.

Lilac followed, weaving in between werewolves and princesses and kids dressed like vampires, Batman, and Scooby Doo.

They darted through a turnstile, each holding up their wrist to the person in the booth, and Lilac did the same.

She followed a ways further until they had caught up with the line. Laughter, screams, and elated energy bounced through a corridor painted bright red. It was as exciting as Lilac had imagined Halloween would be. Maybe even more.

"The Giant Ripper?" Lilac read as she pointed to the sign overhead. "Isn't this the rollercoaster?" She asked, her lower lip and pointer finger a little bit shaky.

"You have to!" Hazel said, grabbing Lilac by both wrists, sensing her trepidation about riding the rickety old wooden roller coaster. "The Giant Ripper is a *tradition*, Lilac! A rite of passage." There was a wild flash in Hazel's eyes and a big smile plastered to her golden, freckled face. "All kids ride the Ripper!"

Lilac supposed she could not argue with such solid reasoning. There were children in line that looked half the age of Lilac, and she was already nine and three-quarters. She couldn't chicken out now, not if it was tradition, and not if those little kids had the guts to do it.

The line moved slowly. With each step, Lilac grew more nervous. The tracks of the roller coaster rumbled and shook as the cars rolled through, and the sound of raving screams fluttered overhead.

Finally, they reached the front of the line. Hazel and Finn began screaming, hollering, and jumping up and down.

"The back of the rollercoaster is the best!" Hazel told Lilac, "The people in the back get more momentum and longer, scarier drops than the people in the front," she explained. "And since we're at the front of the line, we can pick the best seats."

Lilac gulped.

"A lot of people don't like to sit back there," Hazel told her. "But we love it!" Her eyes lit up. Lilac couldn't help but smile. She had to admit, she was nervous to ride the Giant Ripper, but their enthusiasm was contagious.

The roller coaster cars roared through to a stop. A load of screaming, sighing, elated kids got out and ran towards the exit.

The man running the ride waved the line forward. Lilac, Hazel, and Finn plowed through another turnstile. Hazel and Finn ran to the back of the train and got into the second-to-last row.

"Get in the back, Lilac!" Hazel yelled at her.

Lilac hesitated, but there were other kids coming up

behind and it looked like the roller coaster cars were filling up quickly. She trotted to the last row and sat down. Everyone else pulled down the metal bar that held you into the roller coaster. She did the same, and wiggled it as hard as she could to make sure it was really tight. Then the attendant came through and made sure everyone had done it right. She took off her witch hat and held it tightly against the metal bar.

And then the bell dinged three times, the lights began to blink, everyone cheered, and they were off.

Lilac tensed and grabbed on with both hands. The coaster rolled gently down the first hill and through a dark tunnel. It wasn't as bad as she'd expected. She loosened her grip a little. The train of roller coaster cars came out of the tunnel and into the night air. They slowed. The cars jerked. The sound of gears and cranks clacked, and the cars began to go almost straight up, up, up, to the highest peak of the roller coaster. Everyone had quieted a bit.

She held her breath and looked over her right shoulder to the view of the ocean. It was breathtaking, even better than what she thought it might be like from the commercial. The massive gold moon shone over the water and white-capped waves. There were bright lights in thousands of different colors on the rides and buildings all along the beach. She could see the lighthouse in the distance, the same one her mother and father had visited. And the carousel! There it was. Her ears picked up the riveting music of the band organs and calliope bells floating up from the carousel down below. And no signs of Gremory or any sort of ghost capture, she thought. Perhaps she'd been wrong after all.

Her thoughts were broken by the raucous laughter of Hazel and Finn just ahead of her, their voices already hoarse from the excitement of the night.

She looked ahead again and gulped, they were getting pretty high up, and approaching the peak of the roller coaster. Hazel and Finn were holding their arms up over their heads, shrieking, and laughing. She felt the cars slowly lower down into position. So this was what Hazel meant about being in the last car, at the very peak of the roller coaster. Lilac looked downward over the edge, and time stood still for a moment. She got a sinking feeling in her stomach and looked back to the sea.

And there was a ghost. Sitting right there, in the seat next to her, clear as day, his dark swirling eyes locked to hers. He tipped his hat and then held it to his chest.

"Ready to go then?" he said politely.

And the roller coaster plunged.

Lilac held on and she tried to scream, but it was as if all of the breath had been sucked out of her and left behind at the top. She gasped inward in panic, the pressure of her heart and stomach slamming up into her throat at such a velocity that she was certain she would throw up. She wanted to scream. It would feel better if she could just make a sound and scream, but the breath did not come. The roller coaster continued to plunge. When would it end? It would have to end, eventually, unless it plunged straight into the earth. The wind whipped wetness from her eyes, and she hoped they were nearing the bottom. They must be?

Whoosh. The children ahead caught their breath and let out exuberant screams of delight. The roller coaster roared up another hill and tilted to the side around a steep curve.

The screams began again as the front of the coaster headed down another hill. Lilac held on, trying to contain her stomach and heart as she plunged downward towards the earth. She felt the velocity slow a little bit, and she caught her breath. She shifted her eyeballs to the right.

The ghost was still there, sitting right next to her. And he looked as if he was enjoying the ride quite a bit.

She tried to get a better look as she held on, the coaster whipping down another hill. There was a wide, gleeful smile under his handlebar mustache. He wore grease-stained overalls, a handkerchief tied around his neck, and a wrench tucked in his front pocket. He looked down at Lilac and gave her a big smile and a nod.

"I love this part!" He said. "Whooaah!" he yelled gleefully as the coaster went over a series of quick dips.

Lilac smiled. That was actually kind of fun. She felt remarkably free. The sea air rushed through her lungs, and she let out a deep breath and a little holler as they went down a smaller hill.

The ride slowed, and it curved through the end of the track, back to where they started. Everyone was cheering.

"Ah, this one never gets old," the ghost sitting next to her said. "But I've got to get back to work then. Something's amiss tonight." His eyes narrowed. "I can feel it."

The cars jolted to a stop, and the metal bars lifted. Kids began to get up. The ghost stood and motioned to Lilac politely.

"Happy Halloween, Miss," he said to Lilac as he put his hat on, then tipped it to her.

Lilac climbed out.

"H... Happy Halloween!" she said to the ghost a bit shakily, weaving from side to side as she got her balance and put the witch hat back on her head.

8.
Legends and Ghost Lore

"Who are you talking to, Lilac?" Hazel called out to her, giggling hysterically and bubbling over with joy from the ride.

"Oh..." Lilac said, "I just... I just said, 'Holy cow, amazing'!" She smiled at Hazel and tried to look as normal and regular as possible, as if she had not just been talking to a ghost on the roller coaster.

"Did you like it?!" Hazel asked.

"Yeah!" Lilac said, and she was telling the truth. The first drop had been terrifying—but now that it was over, she realized it had been a lot of fun.

"Wooo!" Finn was hollering, holding his hands up over his head and laughing hysterically like he might burst into tears.

"What do you guys want to go on next?" Hazel called out.

"Let's do that one again!" Finn yelled. "This is the

best night of my life!" He screamed at the top of his lungs.

"How about the carousel?" Lilac got up the guts to suggest.

"That's kind of a baby ride!" Finn said to her.

Lilac's heart sunk. But she had wanted to go on it so badly because of her mom's diary and the ghost in the commercial. How could she explain those strange things to her new friends? She couldn't.

"I need some food," Finn said, grabbing his stomach. "I only ate candy and cookies so far today, so I might die," he said to his sister. She nodded her head.

"I could go for a corn dog," Hazel added. "Skully?"

Lilac shrugged her shoulders agreeably.

They turned and darted farther into the Seaside Fun Park, to a nearby food stand. It was painted in bright orange and yellow and had cartoony characters listing all of the different kinds of food you could get.

Lilac looked on in delight at the pictures of "Mister French Fry," the "Turkey-Lurkey Leg," "Electric Lady Limeade," and the "Corn Dog King."

Finn went up to the counter.

"Umm..." He said, looking up at the menu.

"One Turkey-Lurkey-Leg, one giant size Mister Fries, and a limeade...," he looked back at Hazel and Lilac.

"Corn Dog King," Hazel called out. "And a Lady

Limeade!"

"Skully?" Hazel asked Lilac.

"Oh, I'm okay, I don't have much money anyway, I'm..."

"Mom gave us some, it's fine," Hazel said to her. "Get whatever you want,"

Lilac stammered and mumbled.

"Corn Dog King and a Lady Limeade for Lilac!" Hazel called to her brother, taking out the wad of money from her pink-and-purple cowgirl jeans pocket.

"Make that two Corn Dog Kings and three Lady Limeades," Finn said.

Lilac felt a little uncomfortable that Hazel and Finn were paying for everything. But she was also trembling with anticipation and hunger. The smell of the fried, breaded corn dog was mouthwatering. She'd never had a corn dog before, but she'd always wanted one, and she was sure they were delicious. Legendary, even. She'd even given up hope that she'd ever get to try one, yet now it seemed as if she actually might. And she'd never had limeade, either. Lemonade, yes. But not lime.

Hazel and Finn paid and then led Lilac around the corner to a little station with ketchup and mustard.

"I like to get a lot of ketchup," Finn said as he pumped an enormous amount of ketchup into several small paper cups. It dripped everywhere. Lilac filled one small paper cup each with mustard and ketchup. She held one in each hand and waited patiently.

"SEVENTY SEVEN!" A kid in a blue-and-yellow-striped outfit called out of the window at an impressive volume.

Finn jumped up and got a tray of food. He led them into the eating area and through a small maze of tables, arcade games, and gumball machines. They sat down, and the food was divided up between the three of them.

They dug in. The corn dog was even better than Lilac could have ever imagined. It was crispy on the outside but soft inside. It was buttery, greasy, hot and delicious. And it maybe tasted a little bit sweet, like honey. She dipped it in both ketchup and mustard, and couldn't decide which she liked better. The limeade was the most sour and sweet thing she had ever tasted at the same time. It was bright green. It was magnificent.

Finn was chomping hungrily on a gigantic turkey leg. Lilac thought he looked sort of like a wild animal, but it also looked quite satisfying. Hazel grabbed some of Finn's fries, and he tried to stop her. But he eventually relented and shared, and they even offered Lilac some. She had a couple just to try them, but she didn't want to impose after they had already done so much.

Halfway through her delectable corn dog, something caught Lilac's eye. It was a framed display on the wall.

"Haunted History of the Seaside Fun Park," the sign read in bubbly blue letters. There were a series of photographs and newspaper clippings and things beneath. From where she was sitting, she could recognize the pictures of the lighthouse, the carousel, the rollercoaster, and the Tilt-o-Scream. There were a couple of other photographs and some articles written about them underneath.

She had almost forgotten about all of the dire and serious situations in her life, allowing herself to get lost in the pleasures of Halloween and the Seaside Fun Park. But the display of Haunted History sent Lilac twirling back into the lonely thoughts about her father, what the Ghost Guard might be doing right now and the fact that she was desperate to pay homage to her mother tonight by visiting some of the locations from her notebook.

Finn saw that Lilac had fallen into some sort of trance, and looked behind him to see what she was staring at so intently.

"Ha!" he said jokingly, "Figures she'd like all the ghost stuff."

Hazel elbowed him, hard.

"I think it's interesting," Hazel said. "This place has a really crazy, spooky history!"

Lilac widened her eyes and tried to look interested, but not too interested where it might be considered weird. "Oh... yeah?" She said.

"Our cousin Joey Poppins," Finn said suddenly, "he was telling us about some of the hauntings here, and he said they're really real!" His eyes widened back at Lilac and got an excited, yet intense look on his face.

Lilac tried to look surprised, but no one had to tell her that ghosts were really real.

"Like, what?" Lilac asked him.

"Well, the Tilt-O-Scream! He said that's totally haunted! By a lady who died!"

"And the Carousel!" Hazel said. "There's a mysterious lady on the white horse with wings!"

"I dare you to ride that horse!" Finn tapped Hazel playfully on the arm.

Hazel laughed and rolled her eyes. "I'll ride it," She scoffed. "Tonight!"

"I heard it's extra haunted on Halloween!" Finn added. "Everything is!"

Lilac lit up inside. Good. Even if it was just for play, her friends seemed sort of interested in checking out some of the haunted locations that she wanted to visit. And it sounded like they would ride the carousel after all. But would the ghost show up if Hazel was riding on her white horse?

"The Haunted Citadel ride is like... totally haunted, for real," Finn added after devouring more of the turkey leg. "Our cousin Joey Poppins said it's because one of the workers found real human bones that they used for the decorations inside." He took another bite of meat off of the turkey leg.

"From European Vampires," Hazel added. "It's true, it was in the newspaper once when they found out about it."

Finn dipped two french fries in a lot of ketchup and stuck them under his top lip like fangs.

"Blaaaaah! I'm a vampire!" Finn said dramatically. "And my bones will rise tonight!" he joked.

They all giggled, even Lilac.

Lilac wanted to tell them that using real bones as decoration wasn't actually a big deal. The family crest in the foyer of Skully Manor had a real human skull and bones on it, and she knew they were real for a fact. It wasn't some kind of a legend.

And everyone dies, she wanted to tell them, but not everyone leaves right away. Ghosts were real. But she didn't say it. Although Hazel and Finn were warming up about riding some of the haunted rides, Lilac knew she still couldn't tell them the truth about what was going on, and why she had a dead-serious reason to be interested in ghosts.

And how strange, she thought—sitting across a table from the two kids that had bullied and teased her several years ago in the school lunchroom. They had called her a freak, a haunted freak, to be exact. They had known about her home and her family's history, even more than Lilac did it seemed. But tonight they'd bought her food and a special bracelet that got her on all of the rides. And they were discussing ghosts. And they hadn't thrown an apple or a corn dog or fries or any ketchup at her head or said anything mean. Why did they suddenly like her? What had changed? Of all the other kids in town, why did they want to hang out with her, Lilac Skully? But she didn't ask.

She squelched a wave of worry that rose up about the Ghost Guard's mission at the roadhouse. It was followed by another pang of embarrassment over her failed attempt to warn them. The unnerving twinge of loneliness that had followed her for most of her life sprang back up and settled in her bones.

She took another bite of her corn dog and smiled at the sight of Hazel and Finn, who were intently focused on their snacks. And at least she wasn't alone right now, she tried to tell herself. She was actually with friends—real friends it seemed—having fun, doing something normal that regular, un-haunted kids do. And she should buck up and just enjoy it. She *was* enjoying it. Every moment of it. And she would let herself forget everything else and just be a kid. If just for tonight.

They finished their delicious snacks and threw the red-and-white-striped paper trays in the trash.

"I wanna ride the haunted carousel too!" Hazel said. "Let's go, the line's short. And it's not a baby ride, Finn, it's pretty fun, and you get to throw the metal rings in the clown's mouth. I bet I can beat you!"

Finn rolled his eyes.

"*That's* why you don't want to ride, huh, cuz I got more rings in the clown's mouth than you did the last three times." Hazel snickered and clutched her stomach as she made the realization.

"Whatever!" he said. "We'll see about that, I guess there's only one way to know."

An unbounded surge of excitement overtook Lilac as they filed into line for the carousel.

"Which one is the haunted horse?" Hazel asked as they peered through to get a glimpse of the spinning horses.

"It's white with wings, I think," Finn said.

Lilac knew exactly which one it was, even though it was her first time here. She recognized it instantly as it spun around. It was empty. No living rider, no ghost.

"I think that's it," Hazel said as she pointed to it the third time it spun around. "Awww, you can't get the rings from that one. It's in the middle. Skully, you ride it! Ride the haunted ghost horse!" Hazel and Finn

125

giggled.

Lilac smiled and felt a twinge of happiness as she thought back to actually having ridden a real ghost horse just a couple of nights ago. It had been an exhilarating experience. Magical, really.

"Um, okay!" Lilac said, "I'll do it." She shrugged.

The calliope, band organs, drums, and jingling bells came to an end, and the carousel slowed. The riders got off, and the line shuffled forward. As soon as they were through the turnstile, Hazel and Finn took off to secure prime horses for throwing rings.

"Ride the haunted horse, Skully!" Hazel screamed back to Lilac, and Lilac hurried around the carousel to find it.

"Okay," she said under her breath as she spotted the white carousel horse and lifted her foot to climb up.

She smelled a whiff of salt air mixed with something else. Something... hauntingly familiar, yet new and different. The sweet, rooty scent of ghosts mixed with a pale whiff of fine floral perfume.

"Excuse me!" a voice said suddenly. "I was going to ride this horse, thank you very much!"

"Oh!" Lilac stepped back and caught her breath. "It's... it's you!" Lilac exclaimed, as if she knew the apparition. It felt like she almost did at this point.

Ding! Ding! The carousel began to turn, the organs

and calliope sprung to life, and Lilac stumbled to the horse just next to the haunted white one with wings and climbed on.

It was lavender with a bridle full of flowers and gems in all colors of the rainbow. The horse's face was distorted, looking upwards with an expression that seemed quite hideous and painful compared to the gorgeous bridle and fineries and floral motifs of the carousel. Its tongue was out and twisted, its eyes wide and glaring. But something about it was so romantic, Lilac thought. So beautiful. She loved it.

She looked over to the white horse. Sitting side-saddle was a ghost in a striking white dress and a windswept hat with a huge bow of crepe trailing behind it. Her dress was gorgeous, with floral lace and embroidered rabbits and pale pink bows. Victorian, perhaps, with rows and rows of tiny pearlescent beads in a detailed pattern that made it hard for Lilac to look away.

The woman cleared her throat.

Lilac looked up at her. She had a similar look on her face as the horses themselves, although her mouth was closed. It was intense. Possibly painful, yet almost manically staring down at Lilac.

"Do I *know* you?" the ghost woman said.

"Oh, well, no," Lilac said, "But... I know you, well, I

know *of* you..." Lilac tried to explain.

"Very strange indeed," the woman replied, her eyes fixed skeptically on Lilac. She paused as her horse rode up and Lilac's went down. "My name's Mary. Yours?" she said to Lilac as their horses met somewhere in the middle.

"Lilac," Lilac shouted down a bit as her horse rose up.

"A lot of strange things are happening here tonight, not just you, Lilac," the ghost shouted back, then averted her gripping gaze for a few moments.

Lilac tried to think of something to say. "Um... what kind of strange things?" Lilac asked as their horses met again in the middle.

"You know," the ghost replied as her horse rose up again, and she paused 'till she started to come back down. "Of all the years I've haunted here, you're one of the few that's had the decency to talk to me."

"Oh, I think most people are just... unobservant... they're not trying to be rude..." Lilac wanted to tell the woman she'd actually come looking for her, and that her parents were paranormal investigators that had once tried to investigate her, and that she'd actually seen her apparition on a television commercial, but she was cut off.

"So you can see me and others can't, observant little

Lilac," the woman said mockingly. "Well, what makes you so special then? Do you even know? And what are you doing here tonight, dear? Do you have anything to do with *them*?"

"Them?" Lilac said in confusion. "Who?"

"The strange masked men," the woman said in a hushed whisper.

"Oh, well, it's Halloween," Lilac tried to explain. "You'll see almost everyone in a costume tonight."

"I *know* that!" the ghost said as she shook her head. "Not *those* masks," she said as her horse came back down to Lilac's level. "The ones downstairs, in the access tunnels. Men I don't recognize... not the usual crew, if you know what I mean..."

"I... " Lilac felt a pang of worry. Yet any attempts to form a sentence to ask for clarification were cut short by the ringing of the bell, the end of the rapturous music, and the slowing of the carousel.

"I'll try to come ride again tonight," Lilac said as she climbed off of her horse. "I actually have some questions for you..." She looked back up at the white horse, and the ghost was gone. "Hello? Where'd you go?" Lilac said as she looked around.

"We're right here, silly," Hazel said. "I beat Finn again, fourth time in a row," she shrieked and laughed.

"I would have beat you this time, but THREE times

around I didn't get rings! That's just not fair at all." Finn said in his defense.

"Well, wanna go again?" Hazel teased.

"Ok! Yeah!" Lilac shouted back.

"Later!" Finn said. "To the Haunted Tilt-O-Scream!" Finn called out in a spooky voice, lowering his mask back over his face, and leading the way with a stiff, jerky monster walk.

"But..." Lilac tried to protest and get back on the carousel, yet her friends darted off into the crowd, and she had no choice but to follow.

Lilac gulped when they got to the Tilt-O-Scream. It was a massive circular platform that spun around. The people riding stood up against a wall on the very edge of the platform, held in just with a flimsy-looking strap and the force of gravity. You stood and held on while the platform rose up and spun for what seemed like an hour and tilted this way and that. It looked ancient and somewhat horrible. It smelled like grease and diesel fumes. And there was a gigantic, dizzying, and hypnotic red-and-white spiral painted on the center of the platform that got smaller and smaller towards the center. So when the ride spun, it would pull you inward, twisting and warping your sense of reality and perception till you thought you might fall over or barf.

"Whoa!" Hazel said, shaking her head quickly and

looking away from the ride. "Don't look at the center too long!"

Finn chuckled excitedly. Lilac noticed that the sounds coming from the Tilt-O-Scream were different than the joyful screams on the roller coaster, because no one seemed to be screaming joyously. The people riding the Tilt-O-Scream were more or less silent, spinning and spinning around and around on the edge of the gigantic spiraling disc. She heard the occasional whoop or holler blowing down on the breeze and a very faint, occasional cry for help.

"Help! Help!"

Lilac closed her eyes and listened again, closely, but didn't hear it anymore.

Lilac didn't really enjoy spinning. She was worried she'd feel dizzy and sick. But there was no backing down now. She hoped if she went on this ride, maybe she could talk her friends into riding the carousel again.

They waited in line, winding up a staircase that led to the entrance of the ride. Lilac leaned over the rail and peered out to get a better view of the ocean. She had grown up so close to it, but had rarely been to the beach. She regretted that and decided she would spend more time at the seaside from now on, no matter what.

She tried to look around for any signs of Gremory, but didn't see any—not one. She felt silly. She'd been wrong and totally embarrassed herself. Yet the full moon hung high and bright. The cool, salty air chilled the end of her nose. There were hundreds of kids all around, running and laughing in groups, picking which ride to go on next, taking big bites of colorful candy apples. She couldn't allow herself to feel too bad about it anymore, she reasoned. She should just let herself have fun.

Finn pointed out an area a ways down the beach that was roped off. "That's where they set off the fireworks!" He said, his finger waving towards it excitedly. "You can't get too close cuz it might explode! I think I wanna have that job someday."

Then, Lilac saw him again—the ghost from the roller coaster. He was standing across the way, arms folded, his gaze focused intently on something. Lilac followed his line of sight. A man with a white mask and top hat stood up on the turret of the Haunted Citadel. A masked man, just like Mr. Black and the driver of the van. Her heart began to pound a bit as her eyes widened. And the ghost on the carousel had said something about masked men, too.

"Lilac!" Hazel was patting Lilac's arm to move up the line.

Lilac hopped forward to catch up, but she didn't take her eyes off of the man at the top of the Haunted

Citadel. It was Halloween, so surely that meant plenty of people would be wearing that kind of costume and mask... Didn't it? Maybe all of the park security was dressed like that for fun.

They were almost to the front of the line. The towering Tilt-O-Scream had come lumbering down from the sky to a stop. The people exiting from the ride seemed disheveled and dizzy. Lilac felt queasy just looking at them. The line began to move forward as the next set of riders boarded the Tilt-O-Scream.

She felt funny. Was it just her nerves, or something else?

"Help!" Lilac heard. She twisted her head around, but didn't see anyone or hear it again. But she had heard it. Twice now, she was certain.

The line started to move. She got a whiff of something familiar and breathed in. Her nostrils filled with the scents of exotic fried foods, hamburgers, and sugary treats like taffy, funnel cakes, and waffle cones mingled together with the salty sea air and a hint of fish. But those weren't the scents that were familiar. It was something else that she couldn't quite discern.

"Come on, space cadet," Hazel called to her.

Finn remarked that he wasn't sure if they were going to get on the next round of the ride, but the attendant let them on as the last three riders. Lilac stepped onto the gigantic spiraled red-and-white platform, and the ride attendant shut the metal gate behind her. Hazel and Finn sprinted over to two empty stalls. There wasn't a third one next to them, so Lilac ran around trying to find an empty spot. All of them looked like they had been taken. She circled around, the last person to get into place.

She saw two spots over on the far side of the spiral and ran back over. One of them didn't have the safety strap, and had yellow tape crossed over it that said, "Caution" and a handwritten sign that read, "Out of Order." Lilac stepped into the other one and fastened the thin strap around herself. It was far too big for her, and she thought there was no way it would ever hold her in if she were to fall. She gulped and held onto the rails, her witch hat grasped tightly. The attendant came around and checked everyone's strap, but it didn't seem like he checked very well.

Before she had time to change her mind, a whistle went off. Then an alarm bell. Red and white flashing lights. The ride was about to begin. Lilac held on. She closed her eyes and remembered the alarms going off at Black, Black, and Gremory. She had been so close to rescuing her father at that moment! So very close. The hot, burning frustration rose in her, and she tried to forget about it. Just for tonight. After all, the Mulligans and Blue said the Ghost Guard would rescue her father eventually, right?

Her stomach sank. She heard a whirring sound and felt the platform of the Tilt-O-Scream begin to spin. It gained momentum, 'till Lilac felt herself pushed against the wall and frozen into place by the rotating forces.

Then the Tilt-O-Scream began to lift slowly, up, up, up into the sky.

9.
THE GHOST OF THE TILT-O-SCREAM

W*hiiiiiiiiiir.* The Tilt-O-Scream whirred and strained as it lifted the spinning, spiraling red-and-white platform farther up into the air. Lilac felt herself begin to stick to the back wall, her breath knocked out of her as the ride tilted nearly vertically, holding her back as it spun.

The ride made her feel weird. But there was something else. An energetic, magnetic pull that she could no longer deny. What was it? It felt familiar. There was an electrical pulse zapping faintly through the metal bars in her hands. What was it? She closed her eyes again. The red and white lights blinked and bells and whistles clanged. Her mind fell back into the alarms and lights at the laboratory and the electric sparking of the ghost capsules and the horrible orbs. She felt a terrible feeling deep in the pit of her stomach. Something was happening.

"Help!" She heard again, this time so close and so distinctly, she could not ignore it. It was a raspy, terrified, desperate-sounding voice that she wished she hadn't heard.

"Help!" it said again. "Help!" It pleaded, as if almost directly to Lilac. "You're the only one!"

Lilac knew exactly where the voice was coming from. And she knew it was talking to her. She looked to her left. The empty stall of the Tilt-O-Scream wasn't empty. There was a ghost.

The apparition of a woman clutched onto the bars as if for dear life. Her windswept, tangled hair was blown as if she'd been riding the rides for decades. Her face was intense, and her skin looked weathered, a bit wrinkled, possibly from a lot of sun. She wore a tattered sundress, blue gingham with buttons down the front.

"Please!" The woman said to her with moist tearful eyes when Lilac finally got up the guts to look at her directly. "Help us!" the ghostly woman called.

"What's happening?!" Lilac responded, feeling the effects of the centrifugal force and the sparking electricity starting to intensify.

"I can't hold on much longer!" the woman cried. "Something's terribly wrong with this ride!"

"What do you mean?" Lilac asked in terror.

"I've seen spirits!" the woman cried out to Lilac, her

swirling eyes locked open and wide. "More than I can count!"

"Yeah... me, too." Lilac said quietly and nodded her head, just a little bit. She definitely understood how that felt.

"I've haunted this ride for twenty-some years," She told Lilac, "Nineteen, maybe!"

Lilac's stomach began to feel very sick and twirly inside. She'd just wolfed down a very large Corn Dog King and a gigantic tub of Electric Lady Limeade. The ride didn't feel like it was going to stop anytime soon. In fact, it seemed to be speeding up.

"When the Full Moon falls on Halloween," the ghost woman continued, "spirits walk and wander to the Seaside Fun Park, in death, as they did in life." Her voice trailed off a bit. "As the veil thins," she said to Lilac, "And the night wears on to midnight."

Lilac couldn't move because of the force of the ride. But she was also frozen in the gaze and words of the ghost on the Tilt-O-Scream.

"But tonight!" The woman burst out after a dramatic pause that Lilac did not think would end.

"Tonight, the spirits are being sucked into a vortex!" she cried. "Right here, before my eyes,"

Lilac started to shake a bit. The woman's face shook, too, her wrinkles deepening as they spun around, and around, and around. Lilac could not look away.

Lilac stammered. There was so much she wanted to ask, but a dreadful dizziness, a terrible sickness, and a panicky loss of breath began to collect in the depths of her being. She began to sweat.

The woman's eye caught something and she looked away from Lilac towards the center of the ride.

"Look!" She cried, "But don't look too long!" She averted her eyes and shouted back to Lilac. "There's one now! Oh, I can't watch!" The ghostly woman cowered her head down, eyes clamped shut.

Lilac looked towards the center of the ride, and there she saw it. The familiar figure of a ghost spiraling into the center. There one moment and gone the next, into the middle of the spiral.

"You can hear spirits," the woman snapped and whispered almost angrily back to Lilac.

Lilac looked back at her.

"And see," the ghost said, her eyes shifting a bit. "I've been calling all night." Her face squinted up. "Hoping someone like you would hear me,"

"Someone like... me?" Lilac asked.

The woman scoffed. "Know yourself!" she said to Lilac intensely, "and help us! Do something. Tell Roger, the caretaker. He haunts the park day and night, looking for trouble."

The ride began to steady and slow.

"I..." A wave rumbled inside Lilac—the uncontrollable damnation of impending barf which shook her to her core. She would have fallen to her knees if she were not stuck to the wall with the force of the ride. The Tilt-O-Scream spun and spun, finally slowing with each turn. Could she hold on just a little longer?

The ride clanged to a stop, the whistle blew, and the lights on the ride stopped blinking. Lilac unstrapped the little canvas strap and fell forward. She couldn't hold it in, and she couldn't go any further. She vomited. It was dyed a bright green from the Electric Lady Limeade.

"Oh criminy!" She heard the ride attendant say. "Another one tonight? Must be all the Halloween candy..."

"Oh, no!" Lilac heard Hazel and Finn muttering, stifling giggles as they ran over. She felt them pick her up under her arms and hoist her up and out of the turnstile. She tried to move her feet and eventually got her footing.

"That was kind of epic, Skully," Finn said to her in amazement. "Like bright green haunted Halloween barf!"

Hazel giggled uncontrollably, and Finn laughed at his joke, too.

They plopped Lilac on a nearby bench and sat down

on either side of her.

"Are you okay?" Hazel asked her.

Lilac was nauseous, shaking, shocked, exhausted, confused, and totally overwhelmed.

She nodded her head, yes. "Yeah," she said. "Yeah."

"Do you want some water?" Finn asked her. She nodded again. They led her over to a drinking fountain. She drank the cold water and breathed in a bit of the night air. She turned back to her friends and tried to smile through her shivering.

"S... sorry," She said, sheepishly as she sat back on the bench.

"It's ok," Finn said. "It happens. This one time I threw up when..."

Hazel elbowed him. "Want some gum?" Hazel asked as she pulled a pink gum ball out of her pocket.

Lilac nodded and took it.

"Ready for another ride?" She asked Lilac.

Lilac definitely wasn't.

"Um... why don't you guys go on a couple, and I'll meet you right back here in a little while, on the same bench," she pointed to the bench they were sitting on.

Hazel and Finn shrugged and looked at each other in agreement.

"But don't go on the carousel again without me!" Lilac added.

When Lilac was sure Hazel and Finn had disappeared out of sight, she pulled her witch hat down over her face and hurried back out into the crowd.

10.
The Masked Men

The damning implications of what she saw and heard on the Tilt-O-Scream hit Lilac as she walked through the crowd. Everything around her became wonky and blurry, as if she were in her own bubble of space and time.

But was she just imagining it? Was it really Black, Black, and Gremory and one of their plots to kidnap ghosts? Or some desperate attempt by her ego to put together pieces that fit and make her feel vindicated for all of the shame and embarrassment she'd felt in front of the Blue Lady and the Ghost Guard? Yet she'd seen it with her own eyes. And felt it.

And she'd begun to sense something was amiss with the masked men even before she'd talked to the ghost on the Tilt-O-Scream. She wondered if she should get back on the ride and try to talk to her again. She shuddered. She wondered if the ghost ever got to get off the Tilt-O-

Scream. She started to feel queasy again and took some deep breaths.

"She said to find the caretaker, Roger. He must have been the ghost on the rollercoaster." She thought, as he wore grease-stained overalls like a mechanic that worked at a fun park might wear.

Lilac walked to where she'd seen him while she was waiting for the Tilt-O-Scream and circled around, but he was nowhere to be found. She turned off of the main strip and hurried around the back side of the rides. There was a door on the other side of the Tilt-O-Scream, and she jiggled the handle. Locked. Darn. Maybe she should get back in line and ask the ride attendant to stop the ride or sneak up to his control box and do something to disable it.

She turned to head the other direction and was startled by a masked man coming right towards her. She gasped and cowered. He wove around her and approached the locked door she'd just tried to open. He took out a key, unlocked it, and walked through. Just before the door clicked closed, Lilac grabbed the handle and held it open just a crack. A moment later, she slipped inside. She listened to his footsteps plodding down, down, down the metal staircase. She heard a door open at the bottom and then close. She took a deep breath and followed him, as quietly as she could.

At the bottom of the stairs, Lilac took off her witch hat and put her ear to the door, waiting 'till she didn't hear any footsteps or voices on the other side. She opened the door just a sliver and peered in. It was a maintenance tunnel under the Seaside Fun Park, with bare white tile and bright lights. There were short, narrow hallways going in each direction, both left and right. She saw a tool cart on wheels just ahead and dashed over to it. She surveyed the tools quickly.

Wire cutters. Box cutter. Mini-flashlight. Perfect. She grabbed them and then heard a door open down the hall. She dashed back and crouched behind the tool cart.

"Almost midnight!" A voice said with a laugh.

The steps got closer, and she held her breath.

"You know what happens at midnight!" the voice said.

She heard another door open and the footsteps walk through it. Lilac darted forward and scampered in the direction of the door and grabbed the handle, just as it was about to click closed. She opened it just a crack and peered in.

She gasped.

It was an auditorium room with a massive glass tank against one wall. The room was painted blue, with murals of fish and sea creatures everywhere—narwhals, crabs, eels, and barnacles. Rows of bleachers led down to a stage in the middle. It looked like it used to be an aquarium, but there was no water in the tank. It had been retrofitted with a series of wires crisscrossing over it, this way and that, accompanied by a sparking, snapping electrical buzz that Lilac knew all too well.

"Oh, this is horrible!" She muttered under her breath.

It was one of Gremory's ghost snatching orbs. But this orb was much larger than the ones Lilac had experienced before.

There were piles of electrical equipment below the bleachers—antennas going up fifteen, twenty feet with green blinky monitors on makeshift folding tables and electrical cords strewn across the floor. Two men with short black top hats were sitting at one of the tables, their backs to Lilac.

She heard voices in the hall behind her. She slipped into the aquarium room and closed the door with the quietest "click!" she could manage.

Lilac slowly sunk to the ground and ducked into the last row of benches, making herself as small as she could, and peeked over.

"This is terrible!" she whispered to herself under her breath. She could clearly see the souls of six or eight ghosts already trapped inside the tank.

Click. Lilac heard the door behind her open. She flattened herself against the side of the bleachers as much as she could and held her breath. If they looked her way, they'd see her for sure. But they didn't look.

The footsteps of at least three people passed by, then walked down the steps to the equipment at the front of the room. One of the newcomers was talking to the other.

"You're going to love what they've done here," he said with enthusiasm. "With this system we'll be able to capture and contain more spirits in a shorter amount of time than ever before."

"Good." Lilac heard another voice say coldly. "Because this part of the process has been taking far too long."

Lilac could feel the tension fill up the room, even from her distance at the top of the bleachers. She felt an eerie, familiar kind of cold. She recognized that voice. It was the voice of Mr. Gremory, the man who'd kidnapped her and brought her to the Underworld. She held her breath, deathly still, and listened.

"Jerry," the enthusiastic man who had been explaining said. "Tell him why this is such a fantastic plan,"

Lilac peered over the bleachers again, as cautiously and slowly as she could. Jerry, she thought. She recognized his name and face. He'd broken into her house.

"A lot of it has to do with the sheer number of ghosts that we think will be out tonight," he said. "Not only is it Halloween, a time of heightened paranormal activity, it's also a full moon, so we're expecting an abnormally large number of spirits from far and wide to gather." Lilac heard the man named Jerry explain. "And with a pretty ingenious use of some of the existing equipment here," he added, "The spinning motion of the Tilt-O-Scream will act as an energized magnet, and when activated to full strength at midnight, it'll capture the greatest concentration of ghosts in the park." He started to chuckle a bit and had to contain himself. Neither Gremory, nor anyone else joined in his laughter.

"We'll contain a large amount of spiritual energy in a very short amount of time. Brilliant, if I might add," Jerry said.

Gremory looked at the aquarium tank, sparking and snapping with copper rods and straps woven around it. "How are you going to get them from here to my laboratory?" he asked.

"Oh we've got a couple vans coming. They'll be here any minute now, they're retrofitted to transport them. We'll load 'em up into the vans and then bring them over."

No one said anything for an excruciatingly long moment.

"That sounds like something out of... a blasted cartoon!" Gremory's voice bellowed through the aquarium. Lilac shuddered and huddled down into a ball. "What kind of a crackpot idea is that?"

No one said anything. The room was silent. Lilac felt that surely they would be able to hear her heart beat. It was pounding so loudly at this point she thought it might explode.

"It. Had. Better. Work." Mr. Gremory finally said, slowly, distinctly, and angrily, as if each word were its own terrifying sentence.

Then, Lilac heard short, curt footsteps stomp back up the bleachers, followed by the sound of shuffling footsteps.

They were heading in her direction. She flattened herself down again. She had nowhere to go. If she tried to scramble around the other side of the bleachers, she'd be seen. They hadn't looked the first time. She held her breath. Odds were they wouldn't look again. She closed her eyes and pretended to be invisible.

"You!" Gremory's voice gasped.

Lilac did not hesitate. She sprang up and jumped over two rows of bleachers at a time, flinging herself down to the front of the room.

"Get her!" Gremory's voice boomed through the echoey aquarium. The men behind the makeshift tables of equipment jumped up and tried to corner Lilac, but she was too quick. She pushed a stack of equipment with all of her might and sent it tumbling to the floor. She darted through the door on the far side of the room, underneath a bright green sign that said, "Emergency Exit." This was definitely an emergency.

She found herself in another access tunnel and ran as fast as she could. The door from the aquarium opened again behind her, and the sounds of angry men were not far behind.

Lilac slipped through the nearest door, and closed it behind her as quickly and quietly as she could.

"Bwwwahahahha!" Another voice rang out.

She could not contain a bloodcurdling scream as she jumped backwards and then cowered to her knees.

It was Dracula, coming out of a coffin, somewhat robotically, now that she got a glance at it. There were bats flapping around him on a wire mobile apparatus, and little round-top buggies rolling by on the other side.

"The Haunted Citadel!" Lilac said under her breath, realizing where she must be. Her thumping heart rapidly slowed, and she took a massive inhale to steady herself.

She moved into a position where she was hidden in the darkness, just in case the door behind her opened.

She saw an empty buggy roll through the ride and took her chance. She jumped in. Up, up, up the ride went, through a stone hallway decorated with skulls, bones, and gruesome, gory portraits. Two large doors opened with a "clunk," and Lilac's buggy pulled up to the exit of the Haunted Citadel.

11.
The Lighthouse

"Oh, no!" Lilac said to herself in a gasp as she scurried across the boardwalk. "Oh, no! Oh, no! Oh, no!" she repeated, not knowing what else to do. She saw a pink-and-purple hut marked "Security" in black letters and ran towards it.

"Hi there!" Lilac said to the security guard. "Um, there's these bad men here tonight and they've done something to the Tilt-O-Scream. You've gotta stop the ride!"

"What?" the man said. "Where'd you hear this?"

"Oh well, I um... can you just send a security guard down to the old aquarium, please? And have them check it out?"

"The aquarium?" The guard said with a sneer on his face. "You just said the Tilt-O-Scream. Just... just get out of here, kid. Stop causing trouble."

"No, listen!" Lilac said. "They're gonna capture all

the ghosts at midnight and..."

The security guard got out his radio.

"We've got some crazy kid here talking all kinds of jibberish."

"Ugh!" Lilac sighed and ran. She ducked through the crowd, weaving this way and that. She twisted and zigzagged low between groups of people. Her mind and heart raced.

She had been *right!* Her chest burned with rightness. Gremory was at the Fun Park planning something horrible after all. Yet she didn't even want to be right. She'd finally gotten over it and was happy just being a normal kid aged nine and three-quarters on Halloween. Her chin wrinkled and she frowned.

But she had been right! *Argh.* The ghosts of Skully Manor had heard correctly. She wondered what else she was right about that everyone said was wrong. There could be so many things. She didn't even know where to start identifying what was what. This could take a considerable amount of research.

So was the Ghost Guard walking right into a trap? Probably. Yes. Most definitely. She shook her head as she hurried along. She had been right. She couldn't believe it, but yet, she could. Of course she was right. She'd known it. She'd felt it. She had been right all along about so much. And she tried to tell them, yes, she had.

Several times.

Her vindicated sense of rightness was cut off by a sick feeling that Black, Black, and Gremory were up to their same old tricks of capturing ghosts. It was even more horrible than before. And what had he called it? Spiritual Energy? How purely awful. Ghosts were like people, or the ones she'd met were, anyway, not just energy. She looked down at her watch and wondered if she had enough time to try to get to the roadhouse and tell the Ghost Guard. No way she could make it there and back. They'd probably been captured already, anyway. She sighed. It was up to her. It had actually been up to her all along.

She pulled off her witch hat. Something caught her eye up above the Chowder Shack. A masked man in a top hat was peeking over the edge, surveying the crowd. She turned her head away and jumped behind a large adult.

There were a lot of kids in witch costumes, but she needed to get out of hers. She ran into the nearest bathroom and washed all of the green off of her face. She took off the witch's robe and hat and tucked them under her arm. She wanted to ditch the costume somewhere, but since it was Hazel's, she didn't feel right about doing that. She needed a moment to think, and she stepped into a bathroom stall.

She didn't have to meet Hazel and Finn for another half an hour or so. But how would she be able to stop Black, Black, and Gremory and enjoy Halloween with Hazel and Finn at the same time? Surely she couldn't tell them what was going on. Maybe she could find a way to stop Gremory in a half an hour.

She left the safety of the locked stall and peered out of the bathroom, then stepped back into the thick swirling crowds. She moved as stealthily as she could down the strip, glancing back every now and again, hoping not to see the men in white masks behind her.

As she turned her head to the right, a hand grabbed her left shoulder. Hard. She screamed and flailed her arms up. Someone grabbed her wrist. She screamed again and struggled, kicking and twisting with all of her might. It was a strong man with black coat sleeves, but she wasn't able to look at his face or see if he wore a mask. She got a good kick in, and his hand lost its grip. Lilac tumbled to the ground, and she hit the pavement strewn with sand, bits of popcorn, chewed gum, shattered candy, bird poo, and Halloween wrappers. She scrambled forward, feeling the wind of swooping, grabbing arms behind her again as her adrenaline kicked in. She ran, her heart fluttering up into her throat, her head down low among the throngs of people, eyes fixed on the Lighthouse on the far bluff ahead.

The Lighthouse was where her mother and father had done a lot of their paranormal research. And perhaps it would provide some sort of sanctuary, or maybe answers on what to do next. At least it would get her out of harm's way for a bit. Her tired lungs gasped for air. What a mess. It didn't even matter if she had been right about this. This was so big and so much more than she was ready to deal with. How could she stop it on her own?

Even in the throes of her panic, Lilac could not help but notice something curious going on around her. Lilac saw ghosts. More it seemed with each minute, riding rides, standing in lines, and wandering about, enjoying the festive Halloween atmosphere as much as the living. When the ghost on the Tilt-O-Scream told Lilac that spirits from far and wide come to walk and wander there on the Halloween Full Moon, she wasn't kidding.

The cacophony of the crowds—both living and dead—began to dim as she reached the rides for smaller children on the far side of park. It was getting late, and many of the very small children had already gone home. She hadn't seen masked men in several minutes and hoped she had lost them.

Tucked off of the strip, she saw a small round stand

shaped like an apple. It had a glass counter in the front and one person behind the counter. He wore a hat that also looked like an apple—with a little leaf and stem on the top—and a red-and-green-striped uniform.

"Candy Apples, $1.50," The sign read. Lilac felt in her pocket. She had three dollars. Even a little more. She gave a glance behind her and then headed to the candy apple stand.

"One candy apple, please," she said as she handed him two dollar bills.

"What kind?" He asked her.

"Um..." She surveyed all of the magnificent candy apples in the display case. It was so hard to choose. Caramel and chocolate with rainbow sprinkles looked good, but then there was one with chocolate and another with a thick red coating and red sprinkles with chocolate chips.

"What's that one?" Lilac pointed at the one with red sprinkles.

"Cherry Chocolate." The man in the apple hat said.

"I'll get that one, thanks!" said Lilac.

He gave her the candy apple in a white paper bag. She tucked it under her arm, glanced around again, and took off again into the night.

Lilac picked up her speed. The cold, windy air whipped about her. She jogged towards the far end of the Seaside Fun Park and pushed through a tall, creaky turnstile.

The white tower of the lighthouse was just up ahead, brightly illuminated by the light of the moon. What Lilac hadn't seen before was the dark, narrow train trestle that went over a river mouth. It looked like she'd have to cross it to get to the lighthouse. There didn't seem to be any other way.

Lilac walked along the tracks and slowed down, feeling sure that she had escaped the henchmen from Black, Black, and Gremory. She took the candy apple out of the bag and took a bite.

Oh. Wow. It was amazing. The apple was perfect. And the chocolate and cherry coating on top of it was better than she could have imagined. There was a layer of caramel underneath it all. Chewy, soft, and so good. She took another big bite with a satisfying crunch and continued up the path.

She could see a few shadowy figures walking across the train trestle up ahead, crossing both this way and that. The trestle sat under a dark clump of trees on the cliff, lit only by moonlight. She gulped. The footboards on either side of the trestle were narrow, only wide enough for one person to walk. The tall stature of the trestle reminded Lilac of Skully Manor. Faint sounds of music, bells, and merriment from the Fun Park wafted by on the breeze. She stepped onto the wooden planked path, worn to a smooth finish from years of foot traffic.

Plip-plop, plip-plop. Her feet went quickly as she trod. A group of young boys with masks and bags of candy began to cross on the other side of the trestle. They sounded loud and rowdy. She hoped they wouldn't talk to her or try to play any tricks. Lilac strode forward purposefully and didn't look at them. When they approached, Lilac turned to the side to let them squeeze by as the path wasn't wide enough for two people to walk. She took another bite of her apple. They were excitedly talking about all the rides they'd go on and things they'd do and did not give her a second glance. *Phew.* She continued.

She steadied her breath. No one else was coming. She took a bite of her candy apple.

Whoosh. A figure swooped down from the top of the trestle and landed just in front of Lilac, blocking her path.

She tried not show any fear, but she had been startled, and she jumped back.

He was not a ghost, Lilac noticed, not like any ghost she'd ever met. He was solid, like a living person, yet his skin was dreadfully pale to the point that it was bluish. His lips were red, more reddish black and translucent than Lilac had ever seen on a boy. And he had dark-rimmed eyes. Very dark. She wondered if he was wearing makeup, and if it was part of his Halloween costume, or if he wore it all the time. Maybe it was just his thick rows of eyelashes and shadowy, bushy eyebrows. She couldn't help but notice that he was unusually good looking. Yet strange.

He did not say anything, and neither did she.

They stared at each other, him giving her a strange glance through shimmery, shifty eyes. She held his gaze back, determined not to show any fear.

A cold rush swooped through Lilac's guts, and she fought hard not to gasp or flinch. Something was behind her. She turned. Two more pale figures had swirled out of nowhere. A second older boy stood on the trestle, blocking her path back. The other figure was a teenage girl with dark red hair, nimbly perched on the edge of the railing. Lilac saw her face, and she was transfixed by how beautiful, how utterly gorgeous the girl looked. The girl smiled, revealing two glossy, razor-sharp fangs between her blood red lips.

"So, how's that candy apple?" The first boy asked Lilac.

Lilac looked back at him and took a bite out of it without lowering her eyes. "Delicious." She said.

"Are you sure?" He asked her, a sly smile coming over his face, and a mischievous twist on his lips.

Suddenly, the taste of the candy apple in Lilac's

mouth changed, from sweet and delicious to something familiar, salty, and a little bit metallic. Blood. Lilac looked down at her candy apple. It was covered in blood. She looked back up at the boy ahead of her, and as he chuckled, bright white fangs glinted between his lips. Lilac was about to scream, to drop her apple and run, but the taste in her mouth changed back just as suddenly to caramel and cherry chocolate. She looked down at her apple. It was just a candy apple. Just as it had been before.

"Let's go," The beautiful girl said firmly to the first boy. "She's just a little girl," Her figure then leapt off the railing of the trestle and dove, headfirst and arms out, over the side.

Lilac gasped. She listened for the sound of the girl hitting the water, but heard a surprising and eerie nothing.

"Let's go!" the strange girl's melodic voice called out from the nothingness.

The two boys lingered for a moment. Lilac looked back and forth at each of them, uneasily.

"I thought she was one of us," the first boy said, still staring at Lilac. "Look how... pale she is..."

Lilac rolled her eyes. She'd heard that one before. The deathly pale little girl who lived in a haunted house. Very funny.

"Leave her alone," the second boy said, as he jumped over the edge of the trestle.

"Excuse me," Lilac said firmly. "Let me pass... please."

"Where ya going?" he asked her.

"To... to the lighthouse." She stammered, and wished she hadn't said it once she did.

"Oh," he said. "Up to see that nasty old Astrid huh? Kids love to try to get photos of her, but I'd steer clear. She's awful, if you ask me."

"Um... just, please, can you let me pass?" Lilac said.

The man jumped like a cat and landed on top of the trestle railing, then disappeared over the edge.

Lilac let out an exasperated wail. She almost turned around to head back to the park, but there was another group of shadowy figures approaching from that direction. So she started to run. She ran up the dark and steep switchbacks that led to the lighthouse bluff. A few more of the living and dead started down the walkway, headed for the Fun Park. She didn't make eye contact and tried to stay in the shadows as much as she could.

Her lungs were heaving and her legs ached as she reached the top of the hill, but she didn't slow down. The lighthouse was just ahead. She ran across the rocky earth of the bluff. There was a small cottage next to the tower, and Lilac thought she saw a face in the window out of the corner of her eye.

Whoosh! A wave roared up against the cliff.

She ran to the cottage and peered though the curtains. It was dark. She tried the door. Locked.

Whoosh! Another wave roared under the cliffs below. She ran across a lawn and up to the door of the lighthouse tower. She twisted the door handle, expecting it not to turn. But it did.

As soon as the door opened, she had second thoughts. Surely she shouldn't go in. But something told her to go. A longing to discover the place her parents had fallen in love over paranormal research, a place her mother wrote about with such passion. She imagined her mother standing right there. Yet she paused. She held her hand on the door, which was opened just a crack. Then she stepped inside and closed the door quietly behind her.

The lighthouse was still. Deathly still. She closed her eyes. Her resolve and fearlessness faded fast, as soon as she got a sense of the place. The interior of the lighthouse was cold, echoing, dark, and angular from the shadows bouncing every which way off the metal staircase. Lilac took a breath. It smelled salty, rusty, damp, and old, much different than the usual smell of haunting that she knew at home. But there was a familiar, ghostly undertone that Lilac recognized. A mournful yet angry kind of feeling started to creep over Lilac's skin. She shuddered.

She pretended she was her mother. She had to, otherwise she wouldn't have been able to move forward and up the twisting staircase.

Tap. Tap. Tap. Lilac's feet went slowly up the creaking metal spiral stairs, as quietly as she could. Up, up, up, she went. When she reached the top, she held her breath and looked out of the panoramic glass. The view was magnificent.

From the top of the lighthouse, you could see the entire Seaside Fun Park. The roller coaster whooshed by. The screams of the kids flying by on the wind were just audible. The Ferris Wheel swirled with rows of blinking orange and blue lights. And the Tilt-O-Scream spun—the red-and-white spiraling center gripping Lilac in its hypnotic trance. Lilac stopped looking at it. She wondered if Hazel and Finn were on those rollercoaster cars right now, swooping down and having fun. She glanced at her watch in the moonlight. It was later than she'd thought. She had better get back.

She spun around, and her guts recoiled instinctively before her eyes had time to process what was in front of her.

"You!" A ghastly, grayish white ghost rose up. Her hair was stark and matted, long, tangled, and wet with bits of seaweed stuck in the knots. Her skin was peeling down in places like it had soaked in water too long and was beginning to decay. Bones were visible on parts of her hands, arms, and one of her cheeks. Her brow furrowed over high cheekbones and gaping, wide-set eyes, giving Lilac the sense that she may have once been pretty—but now—oh, no. This ghost was dreadful.

The ghost held up an oil lamp on a large metal ring, which lit up her tortured apparition with an eerie green glow. She wore flowing robes in white satin, tattered and wind-torn. An otherworldly wind whisped over her, and the fabric made a sad, ripping, whipping noise, like a lonely flag in the wind, left in some desolate field.

Then the ghost set down her oil lamp and charged at Lilac. Lilac stumbled backwards and around the circular lookout at the top of the lighthouse.

"You think you can sneak in and break my windows and leave your litter and do all kinds of nasty things in here, but I caught you!" The woman screamed at Lilac and chased after her. Lilac ran around the top and tried to get back to the stairs.

"N... No!" Lilac said. "I wasn't going to break anyth..."
Wham.

Lilac was pushed from behind to her knees. She felt a forceful chill and cold rush against her body.

"Liar!" the ghost screamed at Lilac, hovering over

her.

Lilac backed up like a crab on her hands and feet and tried to stand.

"Every Halloween," the woman wailed, "You... merrymakers.... come around here vandalizing my property! Trick or treat! Trick or treat! Trick or treat!" The ghost woman mocked. "But I've had enough!" she screamed.

Her nauseating breath was cold and briny, as if the great depths of the sea were reaching through her, up out of the darkness, making it difficult for Lilac to do any breathing of her own.

"No! I swear! I..." Lilac stuttered, still scrambling backwards awkwardly, trying to avoid the woman's piercing gaze, yet unable to look away.

"I've heard about you!" Lilac said. "In... my mother's... diary!" Lilac suddenly felt very silly.

"A diary?!" The ghost's energy shifted rapidly. She gasped and brought her hands up to her face, tinkling her fingers back and forth. "Me?!" she exclaimed, "In a secret... diary?" She drew the words out in a snide tone.

Lilac nodded. It was more like a paranormal research notebook of musings and a few personal things, but she didn't want to disagree too much.

"What did it say about me, exactly, in this secret... diary?" the ghost asked quietly.

"Um…" Lilac stumbled for words. She didn't want to say the wrong thing, but she also had no idea what the right thing would be, either. So she just spoke the truth, the first thing that came to her head, without thinking.

"It said…" Lilac trembled, "th… that you were a legend!"

Lilac had scrambled once more around the circular top of the lighthouse and grabbed at the railing of the stairs behind her.

"Did it now?!" The woman said with a haughty laugh. "What else?" she asked, a hiss like a sea snake on her lips as she spoke.

According to the legend that Lilac had heard of the Lady of the Lighthouse, she and her sister were in a perpetual argument, even in death, and the mention of her sister enraged the ghost. So Lilac didn't want to bring that part up. She tried to think of something else instead.

"It… said… you…" Lilac stammered, "Sunk ships! On purpose!" She blurted out, hoping this wouldn't anger her.

"Oh yes," the ghost replied with a smile. "That part's all true," she looked back down at Lilac with terse, thin lips, pleased with the recognition of her accomplishments.

Lilac was petrified, but she gave the woman the

friendliest smile she could muster. "So, I..." Lilac tried to say, again in a very pleasant tone. "I ... I liked that story, and I j... just wanted to see if I could find you up here..." Lilac stopped because the ghost was looking at her very skeptically.

"I just wanted to ask you," Lilac said, "um... if that was all true, so... thanks?"

The ghost smiled. "You're very welcome, dear. And what was your name?"

"Lilac." Lilac said, shyly. "Lilac Skully,"

"Skully..." The ghost said slowly, as if she were trying to place it, but it did not come to her. "Astrid." She held her partly decayed hand out to Lilac.

Lilac hesitated, but forced herself to put her hand out. Astrid's cold, fierce, otherworldly fingers gripped around Lilac's hand, and a chill went all the way down Lilac's spine and through her feet. She tried not to give off a visible shudder, but it was hard not to. It made Lilac want to drop to her knees, but she held her ground.

"Nice to meet you, Astrid," Lilac nodded and pulled her hand back as soon as it didn't feel rude or rushed to do so. "I have to go now," Lilac looked at her watch. "Someone's waiting..."

"Happy Halloween, Lilac," The ghost said to her.

"Happy Halloween," Lilac said back and clambered down the metal spiral as fast as she could.

Boom. Boom. Boom. Boom. Boom. Her feet pounded down the stairs. Lilac's trembling hand opened the door, and a whip of salty air hit her lungs. She gasped and began to run, the sound of the waves whooshing and rushing against the cliffs behind her.

12.
THE SEA PIRATE'S COVE

Lilac ran as fast as she could, back across the lawn and rocky outcrop of the lighthouse. She saw a cheap plastic werewolf mask on the ground, and picked it up. It was cracked with a broken elastic strap, but she managed to make it work enough to get it to stay over her face. She realized she'd lost Hazel's witch hat and robe when the man had grabbed her back at the Fun Park. And she'd left the rest of her apple up in the top of the lighthouse, although she'd kind of lost her appetite for it anyway. She looked at her watch. It was almost ten, way past the time she was supposed to meet Hazel and Finn. And her trip to the lighthouse had been perfectly awful and a colossal waste of time. She sighed.

Lilac hurried back down the dark switchbacks and felt a strange, deep rumbling sensation. It got louder and louder, more and more rumbly, as if it were under her feet. Lilac started to panic, not knowing what it was, and imagined a demon coming up from earth to envelop her into the darkness or some terrible kind of poltergeist that was about to crush her living soul from the inside out.

Chuga-Chug. Chuga-Chug. Chug... a... chug.

It was a train, and it was making its way over the trestle. A ghost train. Lilac stopped in amazement and flattened herself in the shadows, against the wall of the switchback trail.

The train had the presence, rumble, and energy of a mighty steam train from the world of the living, but it was clearly otherworldly, with a twinge of a hazy, translucent glow, as if it might disappear if you looked at it for too long. The cars of the train were filled with hundreds of spirits in all sorts of costumes. Some of them were covered in gore and blood, and some of them were dressed up in more traditional homemade getups like strips of fabric for mummies, vampire makeup with capes, and white sheets with eyeholes for ghosts.

Ghosts dressed as ghosts, Lilac thought to herself as she looked on. There were ghosts with jack-o-lantern buckets and treat bags, children of all ages waving out of the train, smiles, cheers, and excited chatter reveling in the vibration and energy of Halloween night. Some of the smaller children saw Lilac hiding in the darkness, and waved out to her. She didn't wave back, hoping to remain unseen. The train full of merrymaking spirits chugged across the trestle and up to the entrance of the Fun Park.

Under her new plastic werewolf mask, she felt a bit more disguised. She crossed the trestle. Her mind raced and she ran, darted, and wove between the living and the ghosts in the crowd. There were now as many ghosts as there were living people. The park was filled with spirits, as lively as the living and all celebrating Halloween. No matter where Lilac looked, she saw ghosts gathered together—some in costumes, some of them not. Many of them looked like they hadn't seen each other in years.

Lilac looked for other people like her, living people that seemed to be able to see the ghosts, but she didn't see any. She looked up at the watchtower of the Haunted Citadel. The masked man was still there. And then she saw another masked man, standing just on the other side of the walkway, scanning the crowd. *Darn it!* With her werewolf mask tight over her face, she did her best to blend in with different groups and families as she went along.

She felt nervous and conflicted. She desperately wanted to see if Hazel and Finn were still waiting for her. But Black, Black, and Gremory were up to something unthinkable. It was clear what she had to do. She swallowed hard and did not allow herself to cry. Friendship would have to wait.

Lilac scurried through the crowds and back towards the Tilt-O-Scream. She looked around at all of the ghosts, just there to have fun on Halloween. They didn't deserve to be captured. She saw the bench where she was supposed to meet Hazel and Finn and peered at it from a distance. To her disappointment and also to her relief, Hazel and Finn weren't there. Lilac looked around, this way and that trying to find them in the crowds, but she didn't see them anywhere.

Just as well, she sighed to herself. She put her hand in the pocket of her corduroy pants and felt the pair of wire cutters. As nonchalantly as she could, she peeked back around the side of the Tilt-O-Scream.

She found a door and jiggled the handle as she walked by. Locked. Darn, she thought.

"Hello there," a voice said behind her. Lilac jumped. She gasped and shuddered.

It was the ghost from the rollercoaster.

"I've been looking for you!" Lilac said. "I think! Are you Roger?"

He nodded slightly. "Didn't mean to startle you, Miss, we sat together on the Giant Ripper?" he said, as if to remind Lilac.

She nodded.

"You're not an ordinary little living one, I can tell," he said to her, politely.

"Um, well, I..."

"Have you got something to do with the men down there?" He pointed to the door.

She looked at him blankly, struggling to find words.

"Do you know what they're doing down there?" he asked her, his hands casually on the hips of his dirty denim overalls.

"No!" Lilac said, "I mean, yes! They're my worst enemies, I'm... I'm trying to stop them! They're plotting to kidnap all the ghosts tonight, and I need your help!"

"Oh my," he said. "Well, this is terrible. On the Halloween Full Moon, too. I've been waiting nearly twenty years for this." He sighed. "Well, by all means then, let me know if I can be of help. I've been sensing something was wrong, but I've never seen anything as strange as I have tonight," he said. "Been working here since the first day the park opened."

"I'm Lilac," Lilac said. "Um... Are you a poltergeist? Can you get me in this door? Their equipment's down there, I have some experience with it and, well, I was going to try to cut some wires or something... or, OH! Could you cut the power to the entire park maybe? Could we do that? Or just stop the Tilt-O-Scream? Tell someone... Or... break the circuits, or... I dunno, like, shut off the power somehow!"

"Hmm..." the ghost thought to himself a bit. "I can open that door for you, that's for sure. As for cutting the power or stopping the ride... give me some time to think. Let me see what I can do." He gave Lilac a wink and a reassuring nod.

She felt a glimmer of hope. The door swung open on its own.

"I'll go rile up some of the other spirits here and keep an ear out. If there's any trouble, I'll come find you," said Roger.

Lilac nodded, hesitated, and then hurried inside the door.

She ran down the twisting metal staircase and rounded two corners. There was a set of double doors at the bottom. One of the doors opened. Lilac was face-to-face with two masked men.

Both Lilac and the men froze and gasped at each other in horror.

"You!" one of the men said in disbelief.

Dang it. They had recognized her, even in the werewolf getup. She twirled around and ran up the stairs.

"Get her!" They yelled as they ran after her. Before they had time to catch her, she flung herself over the bannister and back down to the double doors. She slammed her shoulder into the door and ran through as fast as she could, into the brightly lit maintenance hall under the Fun Park. It all looked the same, a series of tunnels and access doors to the different rides, restaurants, and stands. There was a hum and a whir coming from the powerful motors of the rides in the distance and a minuscule but unnerving pulse to the lights and electrical current.

She ran as fast as she could, but heard the door and the sound of the men chasing her seconds later, just behind her in the echoey tile hall.

"It's that.... confounded little girl again, dammit!" She heard one of the men yell.

"Stop her!" they shouted.

"You're kidding me!" A voice called back over the radio.

Lilac took a hard right, then found another long parallel hallway with numerous doors and hallways on either side. She took another right around that corner and slipped into the most random and unassuming door she could find. She looked around. The lights were off, the partially underground room only dimly lit from the skylights and windows way up high, letting in just a narrow flood of moonlight from up above. She saw the unmistakable outline of a pirate ship.

"The old mini golf," She said to herself, realizing

where she was. She ran stealthily and quickly, without thinking, and hoisted herself up the mast of the pirate ship, to the top of the crow's nest.

She waited. Nothing. Then, with a bang, the door she had entered through was flung open.

She smushed herself down as far as possible and held her breath.

"God, she could be anywhere!" She heard a voice yell as they waved a flashlight beam around the dark pirate-themed indoor mini golf course.

She had to stifle a laugh.

The men left and the door closed. Lilac waited a few more moments in silence. Then she let out a heavy sigh and sat back. She felt incredibly strange all of a sudden, like she was not alone. She looked to her left, and her stomach sank.

It was the ghost of a pirate.

"Shh!" the pirate smiled cheekily and held a finger up to his lips. "Ya think they're gone yet?" he asked her, a twinkle in his eye.

Lilac didn't say anything. She stared at him for a moment. She realized she was still wearing the werewolf mask.

"Yes...," she finally said. "I think they're gone." She whispered as she took off the mask.

"Name's Captain Barnabas," he said, as politely as a

pirate could. "Barnabas Butkus." He nodded his head. "Nice to meet ya, Lilac," he added. "Someone's chasin' after you, too, huh?"

"Yes," Lilac replied with a bit of a smile. She looked at him and squinted one eye. He was a ghost alright, a little bit translucent, that unmistakable bluish glow that most people can't even see at all. He was decked out in full pirate regalia, and it looked real—dirty, rough, and sea-worn. Not like one of those cheap costumes that Lilac had seen on some of the other kids, or on some of the employees at the park. Those looked fake. His long beard had braids, ribbons of gold, jeweled beads, and shells woven through it, and he wore a string of giant pearls and shark's teeth around his neck.

"Are you the ghost of a... real pirate..." Lilac couldn't help but ask him, "Or the ghost of someone dressed... in a pirate costume for the... golf course?"

He laughed and scoffed. "Well, I'm a real pirate!" he said. "Real as you get for a ghost, anyway. Does this look like some dreadful costume to ya, girlie?" he pulled the hook off his hand, revealing a gnarled, ghostly stump of an arm.

Lilac gasped.

"Bull shark," he explained. "Then I had to cut it off me'self," He winked back at her, plunking the hook back on.

Lilac couldn't help but smile a bit. She wondered how long ago he'd sailed those very seas. Where had he traveled? What was the world like then? Two hundred years ago, maybe? Three hundred? The dirt and grime and hard sea living mixed with the pungent scent of crab cakes and rum were present, even though he was an apparition. She wondered what the name of his ship was and where he'd sailed. She thought of so many questions.

"How'd you end up haunting the old Pirate Mini Golf?" she asked, hoping it wasn't rude.

The pirate looked at her blankly for a moment.

"Pure ungodly coincidence, Miss." He responded seriously.

Lilac was not sure what to say.

He burst out laughing. "Fitting, innit?" He said. "Me plundering ship was sunk here long ago. I went overboard, and I got bit by a great white." He pulled up the bottom of his shirt, slightly. Lilac gasped at a series of deep, red shark tooth marks across his belly and side. "Swam to shore, only to die of blood loss just as I made it in," the pirate continued. "Real tragic-like," he said, his eyes moistening.

"And here I haunt." He paused for a moment.

Lilac waited for the piece of information that would tie it all in to the pirate-themed mini golf course.

"Few hundred years later, they built this very ship and golf course over me haunting spot!" the pirate finally told her, waving his hooked hand around the room.

Lilac looked at him, incredulously.

He smiled, and his eyes twinkled.

Lilac couldn't help but laugh. She let it loose, and he chuckled with her.

"And that's the short version of me death and me haunting life so far," he said with a chuckle and a sigh. "But it goes on and on. And now they've closed this here mini golf and are talkin' 'bout tearing out me ship," he said solemnly. "And if you want to hear about me childhood days, get out yer handkerchief, missy, you be good and ready for a tale o' woe...." He shook his head.

Even though she didn't know his story, she felt like she might understand. Her childhood felt very sad at times, too.

"Tis a sad one, a terrible tale, and so strange, ya wouldn't believe me if I told ya!" the man continued. "You'd call me a liar."

Lilac nodded her head vigorously in understanding. She knew exactly how that felt, for sure.

"I... I know just how you feel, I think!" she said to him. "I mean... no one ever believes me." She started to cry.

"Oh," the pirate said to her. "It's alright, ya wee little wench. Everyone's got a tale o' woe!" he continued, soothingly. "And ya gotta tell it, sometimes, as sad as it feels, as much as it feels like burning salt water and sand in your eyes and a fish bone stuck up in yer throat as the words come out," He said. "Because you'll feel better, after," he tried to convince her, "Even though your story may be dark at times," he whispered, "so dark. And stormy." He paused dramatically. "But, even the dark o' night will end with the rising sun at dawn."

Lilac just sat there and cried. He was right, she thought. The tears did feel like burning salt and sand in her eyes.

"And it's ok to confide in friends," he said. "Even if ya feel real dark, or ya did bad deeds and plundering," he told her. "Honesty's a pirate's best policy." He stopped, and corrected himself. "Err... well, no. No, not always, but um... Honesty," he stated carefully, "it's real good sometimes. Especially when it comes to matters of the heart."

"I, I didn't do anything bad," Lilac broke out from her sobs and explained. "I don't think I've plundered either... recently, anyway..."

The pirate got a funny look on his face and paused.

"I mighta!" he laughed heartily again, nudging to Lilac.

She smiled a little and sniffled.

"Anyway," he said. "You've heard my tale o' woe, or a bit o' it, now what's yours?"

"I...," Lilac said. Where would she start with her tale of woe? Her whole life had seemed desolate, lonely, and woeful.

"My name is Lilac Skully," she said, a quizzical look on her face, as if she was asking a question. "And I grew up in a haunted house," she whispered.

The ghost looked at her, wide-eyed, a smile appearing on his lips. "Skully huh? That's a pirate's name if I've ever heard one. Is that your real family name or your plunderin' sea name?"

"Oh, it's my real name," Lilac reassured him. "Lilac Skully."

"Sounds pretty good to me so far," he said to her and motioned for her to continue.

"A few weeks back," Lilac said, cutting to the chase of her current problem, "my father was kidnapped!"

The pirate scoffed and shook his head, as if to sympathize. "Ain't right!" he added.

"And then I found out that the same terrible men are kidnapping ghosts from all over!"

"Kidnapping ghosts, little Miss?" he asked her with a gasp.

"Yes," Lilac said to him solemnly. "They're the

sworn enemies of my family. And even worse, they're kidnapping more ghosts here tonight!" She looked at her watch. It was already ten thirty. "At midnight," She told him, "Hundreds! You, too! All of the ghosts here!" Lilac raised her arms dramatically.

"Great Scott and good Lordy Jedediah...," the pirate said. "I knew there were somethin' fishy happening tonight...," he said, thinking very hard. "Been feeling a strange sensation on the wind..."

Lilac told him all about the Tilt-O-Scream and the machinery and the ghost capture orb in the old aquarium. She told him about the men in the white masks and the hundreds of unsuspecting ghosts arriving by the minute.

"Their organization's name is Black, Black, and Gremory," Lilac said to him, her eyes fixed and determined.

"And I've got to stop them," she whispered.

13.
CAPTAIN SKULLY

"Well, ya got me on board," Captain Barnabas said to Lilac, all fired up. "There's no way they're sucking me into their terrible machine after three hundred and sixty two-something years o' haunting."

Lilac gasped. Three hundred and sixty-two years! Amazing.

"Bad enough they're talkin' about tearing down me ship here. Takin' out me golf course! My only sanctuary!" He seemed distraught.

Lilac could see there was already some demolition going on in the old mini golf course. Some construction materials had been brought in and were stored in the corners and open spaces.

He waved what would have been a pointer finger on his one hand around the room, but it had been cut off, down to the last knuckle.

Lilac tried not to stare at it.

"Wee bitty nurse shark bit it right off," Barnabas said, explaining his missing finger when he saw Lilac trying not to look at it. "That sure was stupid. Not me best day, anyway," he laughed.

Lilac gave him an innocent grin.

"So what do we know about the enemy ship, Captain Skully?" Captain Barnabas asked her.

"Well, the orbs and ghost capture devices work using electricity to trap the spirits." Lilac said. "And I've done things like cut the wires or break the circuit or the suction device to disable them." She thought back, "And, I've smashed through the glass also, but that was quite difficult."

"'Lectricity's the devils work!" The pirate said with a ghastly expression erupting over his face. "Sunk me ship right out past the kelp beds, she did! The Lady O' The Lightning!" The Pirate pointed out over in the direction of the sea with his missing finger. "T'was a terrible dark deed!" the pirate said in a vengeful voice.

Lilac shrunk back.

"Sorry, Miss," the pirate apologized, trying to contain himself. "Didn't meant t'scare ya but I'm.... I'm still angry at that woman!" He shook his head. "Sank me ship! Off shore! From the lighthouse!" he said in disbelief. "On purpose!" He held back tears.

"That's awful," Lilac said to him quietly. "Do you mean the ghost in the lighthouse?" Lilac asked him. "Astrid? The one that still haunts there?"

The pirate stayed silent, his eyes moist. He looked down solemnly, then up into the sky. "Yes," he said slowly with contempt. "You've told me about your worst enemy. She's mine."

Lilac shivered. "Well, that's a coincidence," she said quietly. "I... I just saw her tonight." Lilac suddenly felt scared. She hoped the pirate would not react in anger towards her.

"Didja!" he scoffed. "And is she as lovely as ever?"

"Pretty awful really," Lilac said, remembering how she'd yelled and hissed and waved her decaying arms about, chasing Lilac around the top of the lighthouse.

Lilac's expression fell, imagining it all. Then her eyes widened. "Lightning!" she exclaimed.

"Where?" The pirate ducked in horror.

"If we could get lightning to strike, and... we could send a surge through the equipment and blow out all the electricity at the park!" Lilac stuttered, trying to explain what she'd just thought of. "Or if we could break through the glass on the aquarium somehow..."

"Well, for breakin' things, a cannon's the best way to go." the pirate added, quite practically.

"Is there a cannon here?" Lilac asked him.

The pirate sighed. "Yes, but I've not been able to use it since they brought it in, and there's no gunpowder that I know of," He pointed to one of the mini golf course holes that used an old cannon and a pile of cannon balls as part of the scenery. "Those kegs are just empty!" He scoffed at a pile of decorative—and apparently empty—gunpowder kegs.

"What are those? Spools of wire?" Lilac asked, pointing towards some of the construction materials that had been stored near the cannon.

Captain Barnabas's eyes widened and he shook his head. "Not sure, Miss, some kind of sorcery and snakes they've brought in here to destroy me ship, me thinks..."

Lilac tried to nod sympathetically. It looked to her like they were large spools of electrical wire for construction, but she wasn't quite sure, given she wasn't an expert on such things.

Lilac climbed down out of the crow's nest as quietly as she could and went over to the cannonballs. She tried to lift one up. She could barely pick it up a half an inch off of the ground.

"Ugh," she said. There was no way she could lift one into the cannon by herself.

She went to the big spools of wire. She could barely move them.

"And you're not a poltergeist?" she asked Captain

Barnabas.

"No, Miss," he replied.

"Do you know any at the park?" she asked him.

"Well, Cap'n Roger Melmac oversees the park, he's... not your strongest ghost, but he's got a few tricks up his sleeve. A good man."

"Yes, I've met him," Lilac said. "Hopefully he'll meet us, he said he would..."

"And that dame... what's 'er name... on the horse...," he said. "Got a bad habit of slapping naughty folk out on the boardwalk. Never seen 'er lift a finger to move somethin' heavy like this, though."

Lilac was deep in thought.

"What ya got on yer mind there, Captain Skully?" the pirate asked. "What ya thinking?" he asked her.

"We could run this wire," she said with a light in her eye.

"From the weathervane on the top of the Haunted Citadel!" she realized suddenly. "And wire it up to the equipment in the aquarium and have Astrid strike it with lightning!" Brilliant! That might actually work! But she'd never be able to carry it all the way by herself. She thought about her friends.

"But..." she was flustered and panicked, putting her head in her hands for a moment. "Aaah!" She let out a wail.

"What is it, wee little pirate Skully?" Barnabas climbed down from the crow's nest and crouched down.

"Tell me yer troubles now. Feels good to talk about it, from time to time, ya know,"

"I was having so much fun with my friends!" Lilac wailed. "It was my first Halloween!" she cried. "And I've never had friends! Or any fun! And now my friends will think I've ditched them," she blubbered, "because I have."

She cried as the words wavered out, barely audible, and she tried to catch her breath. "Even though I want to go on more rides and hang out with them all night," she said. "But someone has to stop Gremory and save the ghosts!" Lilac cried and looked at her watch again. "And I'm running out of time!" She wiped her nose on her sleeve. "I can't do both at once."

"Well," the pirate said and thought to himself—hard. "If they're any kinda true friends, I'd say they'd understand at least. And at best, they'd want to help ya save the ghosts! Well, you've got me all riled up about it, and I want to do what I can and help ya save the night..."

Lilac thought about the card at the fortune teller's shop. It was the card of friends, and it showed three friends, to be exact. She'd thought it had meant Blue, but maybe it was supposed to mean her, Hazel and Finn?

"Thanks," she said to him.

"Lemme tell ya one more thing," the pirate said to her, his hook raised. "A pirate isn't always known for being the most social-like, if you know what I mean,"

Lilac nodded. She supposed he was right about that.

"But if ya notice, Miss Captain Skully, we pirates most often roam the seas in numbers," he said to her with a smile. "In a crew!" he said.

"Because..." he said extra slowly, as if he was putting together his reasoning right there on the spot, "like it or not," he continued, "when we roam the seas together, we got a better chance of surviving." He looked at her solemnly. "It's the gosh darn truth. And," he laughed a little, "it's more fun to drink rum and plunder together!"

Lilac laughed, even though she wasn't sure if he was serious or not.

"Gets lonely on the high seas all by yerself sometimes, don't ya think?" he asked.

Lilac nodded. She definitely knew about being lonely, as much as she didn't want to admit it. The stark contrast of what it felt like to be with friends had made the loneliness of her life plainly clear tonight.

"But, my friends won't understand..." she blurted out her true fear, as silly as it felt. "They can't see ghosts like me... and... they either won't believe me or..." she didn't want to say it, but she did. "They'll think I'm weird. Crazy."

"Well," the pirate thought deeply again. "Everyone's got a little something that's weird and different about them. Some of it's obvious, some of it's not," he said. "For example," he continued, "it's obvious I've got a gnarled arm." He pulled his hook hand off again. "And I'm missing this finger. But I've also got this glass eye, hidden conveniently under me patch." He popped out his glass eye. "See?" He said, then stuck it back in and put the patch back over. "No one'll notice."

Lilac smiled.

"And," he said, "I wrap me legs and arms in seaweed from time to time. It's good for me circulation. But none of the blokes on the ship ever understood. Said I was strange..." he muttered and looked off, reminiscing. "Sometimes things like my eye popping out or my hook arm makes people uncomfortable, but that's how ya knows its yer real friends!" He shrugged. "And if they ain't yer real friends..." he said. "It's better to find out sooner than later."

Lilac supposed he was probably correct.

"When they still tolerate ya, and they stay on yer crew. That's how ya know. Then they'll help ya when seas get rough. And they'll lend your their arms when its time to load the cannons," he added.

Lilac thought about that for a moment. She thought about Hazel and Finn, and how much she wanted to be with them right now.

"Maybe I can go find them," she said. "My friends, and tell them the truth," she gulped. "Ask for their help," She felt cold inside. "Or at least just tell them the truth."

He nodded at her, encouragingly.

"Okay," Lilac said and looked at her watch. She couldn't hesitate. It was now or never.

"I hope I can find them," she said to Captain Barnabas. "It might be too late…" she added hesitantly. "I might not find them and…"

"Best o' luck to ya, Captain Skully," He replied.

"I'll be back either way," Lilac said to him and gulped. She went back to the doors and put her ear against the wood to listen. Nothing. Lilac cracked the door open a bit, and not seeing anyone up ahead, snuck out and up the stairs, and into the crowds of the Fun Park.

14.
TRUTH AMONGST FRIENDS

Lilac went back to the bench where she was supposed to meet her friends and looked around. She wanted to stand up on the bench or call out their names, but there were still masked men stationed all around, and she didn't want to call attention to herself. She didn't see Hazel and Finn anywhere, and her heart began to sink.

"Lilac!" she heard from behind her suddenly. She turned around.

It was Hazel and Finn!

"Where'd you go?" Finn asked, annoyed. "We've been looking all over for you instead of like, having fun and going on rides."

Lilac did not respond. She pulled up her plastic werewolf mask and looked at them in the eyes, heat rising up from her neck into her cheeks and face.

She felt so ashamed. But she didn't know how to

tell them. How could she say that she could talk to ghosts, and that, in the last hour, she'd seen one at the lighthouse and talked to several more? How could she say that she was the only person that could save the ghosts of the amusement park and that there was an evil plan right now to capture hundreds of spirits. How could she explain all of that?

"What is wrong with you!" Hazel burst out. "Why won't you tell us what's going on? Where were you?"

Lilac still was at a loss for words.

"Lilac!" Hazel called out again, exasperated.

"Let's get out of here, Haze. This kid is too weird," Finn said. He took his sister by the arm and started to lead her away. Lilac froze. She wanted to run after them, but how could she? They would never understand. It was no use trying, she thought. But she remembered what the cards said. And the pirate. That she needed her friends. And the way to know if they're really your true friends is to tell them the truth. And she wanted real friends so bad, she just had to know if they'd still like her despite the truth. Even if it was for the worse.

"Wait!" Lilac cried, her voice sticking in her throat terribly, enough that no one could hear her over the crowd. "Wait!" She yelled again. "Hazel! Wait!" She cried through tears and ran after them. "Finn!"

Hazel tapped her brother's arm and motioned for

him to stop.

"I have to help the ghosts, okay?" Lilac called after them. "And stop my family's greatest foe, Black, Black, and Gremory," she said through tears, choking out the words. She spoke as clearly as she could, but realized how hideous her face must look and how jumbled her words must sound though her deep, heavy sobs. It took every ounce of her energy to say the words. She bent over and rested her hands on her knees, unable to hide her tears. Hazel and Finn said nothing. They looked at each other.

"Ghosts?" Finn asked.

Lilac couldn't speak. Yes, she nodded her head furiously, eyes pinched and tears flowing down her face. She covered her mouth with one hand.

"Are you like...," Hazel paused, "some kind of ghost whisperer or something?"

Lilac didn't know. She shook her head and began to cry more.

"Why didn't you tell us?" Finn asked.

"I'm... I'm so weird!" Lilac sobbed. She tried to continue. "I didn't think you'd understand. I didn't think you'd want to be my friends if you knew all of this." She felt like she couldn't breathe.

"My father was kidnapped," she tried to tell them between sobs. "He doesn't have the flu. And I uncovered a plot tonight," she told them, her eyes as wide as saucers, wet with flowing tears. "A terrible plot tonight to kidnap all the ghosts here, hundreds of them at midnight." She motioned her arm around, Hazel and Finn's heads followed it, trying to see what she saw.

"And... I just want you to like me! To be my real friends." Lilac burst out, crouched down to hug her knees. She felt so stupid saying that. But it was true. She just wanted them to like her. The real her. Whoever that was.

"No one's ever wanted to hang out with me before!" she cried.

After she said this, she wasn't sure if the pirate was right. He said it would feel good after she told her feelings, but she felt sick, and worried and terribly vulnerable.

"And I don't understand," Lilac wailed. "Are you really my friends? And why all of a sudden? Why now? I thought you hated me since first grade."

Hazel and Finn were silent for a few moments as Lilac sobbed. They looked between each other, uncomfortably.

"Well we're the kids with Psycho Dad," Finn said suddenly. "I guess you're the ghost girl from the haunted house and we're the kids with Psycho Dad. That's why we're friends." There was a slight twinge of emotion in his voice, which he swallowed.

"What?" Lilac sniffled and looked at him.

Then the seemingly strong and infallible Hazel began to cry, although she was trying as hard as she possibly could to stifle the tears welling up in her eyes and throat.

"Yeah, didn't you hear about our Psycho Dad?" Finn said. "I thought everyone did, everyone at school did, anyway, I guess you're the only one that didn't know. It was in the newspaper, too, but they didn't use our names. Still everyone knew it was us."

Hazel finally couldn't stop and let out a sob. Finn put his arm around her like she was his beloved teddy bear.

Lilac hadn't heard about that. She didn't typically read the newspaper, and. of course, she hadn't been to a school in a very long time or out much in the community.

"No, Lilac said quietly. "I didn't hear and... I'm so sorry...." She wasn't quite sure what he meant by Psycho Dad, but it was obviously a difficult subject for the twins.

In one long breath, with his arm draped calmly over his sister's shoulder, Finn tried to explain. "So that's the truth," he said painfully. "Yep. None of our friends would come to play anymore, even Hazel's best-best friend Jessica Black, and their moms wouldn't let them see us anyway. They almost didn't let us play on the soccer team, but they had to because we're the best players.

They kept losing without us, and they were gonna get kicked out of the league. Still none of the kids want to talk to us anymore because everyone's afraid of our dad. He's crazy. He escaped from the mental institution and broke into our house and beat up our mom, and then he went out on the run. Now there's a warrant for his arrest and the cops are looking for him and.... We hafta do homeschool... and..."

Hazel took a deep breath and put her arm out to him. He stopped.

"I'm so sorry," Lilac said, taking in the story. It all made sense. Why they'd been so mean and their sudden change. The awkwardness at the door of Jessica Black. And why they didn't seem to have any other friends either. "You guys must be so scared," she said.

Hazel looked at her brother and then at Lilac.

"We were, but sometimes things are just so scary for so long, after a while, they just aren't as scary anymore." She shrugged. "It still makes me sad, but life goes on." Hazel sighed. "And you can't just live in hiding all the time."

The twins looked at Lilac, and Lilac looked back at them.

"I know what you mean," Lilac said in barely a whisper. Lilac had lived most of her life in hiding. And she was just starting to process all of the wonderful things that she'd missed.

"Mom wouldn't let us go to Halloween last year," Hazel said, recalling the injustice. "And after that, I... I said... never again. Never again will we miss Halloween." Her greenish-brown eyes shimmered under her tears. "It's just not right."

"So, do you still want to hang out with us?" Finn asked Lilac.

"Yes!" Lilac said, stunned. "Of course I do!" She nodded vigorously. "Do you still want to hang out with... me?" Lilac said.

They both nodded.

"Okay," Lilac said, stumbling and pushing herself hard to say what she needed to say, "The only thing is, right now I have to go meet up with the pirate... ghost... in the old mini golf course, and um... we need to try to stop the ghostnappers from capturing all the ghosts at the stroke of midnight..." Lilac listened to the words come out of her mouth. They sounded so ridiculous. "Do you guys want to come with me? It's dangerous," she told them, "But, I could really use... help," she said with a timid smile.

Her friends looked at each other eagerly and back to Lilac.

"We wanna help save the ghosts!" Finn exclaimed.

Hazel agreed. She seemed excited. "And we want to

help you!" she said.

Lilac looked at them with a new glimmer of hope in her wet, red eyes. They really understood! And it was crystal clear that they were really her real friends! Lilac felt as good as she had ever felt in her entire life. The pirate was right. She'd told her feelings to her true friends, and it hurt, but then magic had happened.

"Do we get to see real ghosts?" Finn asked.

"Um... they're all over here tonight." Lilac looked around. "I don't think everyone can see them exactly, but I'll try to show you and point out where they are when I can."

The twins nodded.

Lilac hesitated for a moment, waiting for someone else to lead. She looked at her watch. Almost eleven. It was up to her. She lowered her werewolf mask and dashed off, leading her friends through the crowd.

15.
THE SECRET OF THE SISTERS

L ilac cautiously approached the door to the underground access tunnels that she'd used to exit the Sea Pirate's Cove. No one had been there moments ago, but there was a masked man there now, guarding the very same door she'd escaped through.

"Shoot," she said as she held her friends up behind her, hiding around a corner. "See him?" She said to them. "That's one of the masked men," she whispered.

"Just like Jessica's father," Hazel said.

Lilac didn't know Hazel and Jessica Black had been such close friends. It felt like Hazel was still quite upset from the sudden breakup of their friendship especially since it wasn't Hazel's fault, Lilac reasoned. Hazel's eyes narrowed.

"Is there another way in?" Finn asked Lilac.

"Yes, but it's not quite as straightforward," Lilac said.

They shrugged.

Lilac knew they had no time to waste. She led them back into the crowds. They ducked around and checked the access doors by the Tilt-O-Scream.

"Drat," Lilac said. "There's a guard there too. But that seems to be their main entrance," She noted. Her mouth twisted. "I've got another idea!" Lilac said as a mischievous smile came over her face.

"What?" Hazel and Finn asked her simultaneously.

"Come on!" She cried out and ran off into the crowd, the sound of her friends' quick footsteps following behind her.

Lilac led them into the entrance of the Haunted Citadel ride.

"The Haunted Citadel?" Finn asked. "Do you know a ghost in there, too?"

"No," Lilac said, leading them through the twisty ropes and poles. "But there's a way in that I think no one will be watching."

They got in line for the ride. There was a long wait. With the clock ticking down till midnight, every minute spent in line seemed like an eternity.

Lilac tried to quietly point out some ghosts in the crowd. "Across on that bench," she said, "a man and a woman sharing some french fries." Hazel and Finn squinted their eyes in that direction. The line inched forward.

"Ugh... what's taking so long!" Lilac said.

"Psst!" She heard behind her. It was Roger, the caretaker ghost.

"We're trying to get back downstairs," Lilac whispered. "Can you make this line go faster?" She asked him.

He raised his eyebrows and smiled.

Suddenly, a warning bell rang at the front of the ride, and all of the cars stopped. Everyone in line moaned.

"This way!" Roger said to Lilac as he unhooked a metal chain. Lilac waved her friends through. They went through an access door and through a short tunnel that looked like the rock of a haunted castle, with skulls and bones and eyeballs and things set into the stone. There was an empty buggy for the ride, all ready to go.

"Hop in!" Roger said, and Lilac got into the seat. She waved her friends over and they followed.

"Meet us downstairs if you can," Lilac told Roger, "With Captain Barnabas in the mini golf, we need all the help we can get!"

He nodded.

The metal bar of the ride lowered into position. The alarm bell rang again, and the ride clunked back into motion. Roger waved them off.

"Bwhahah!" A speaker in their buggy said. "Welcome

to the Haunted Citadel!"

Finn burst out laughing hysterically, and Hazel followed. Lilac started giggling, too. Although the situation was actually quite serious, she couldn't help but see that the idea of a fake haunted ride for fun was funny, especially with all she'd been through lately. There was also that fact that she'd grown up in a real haunted house.

They rode past a door with a grated cell, remarkably like the one Lilac had been locked in when she was taken to the Underworld. A skeleton popped up and wailed.

Hazel and Finn screamed, and Lilac shuddered in terror, her breath escaping her. Hazel and Finn started laughing again, and Lilac tried to regain her composure.

Their buggy then pulled into a patch of darkness and swirled down, down, down, down a spiraling track and into the underground depths below the Fun Park, into the darkness of the Haunted Citadel. The buggy jerked forward and around a bend.

"It's too late to turn back now! Bwahahah!" said the voice of the ride.

Two large doors swung open, and they emerged in a room decorated like a haunted forest, with bats and ghosts in luminescent paints, standing out brightly against the black walls and blue lighting.

"Hoo! Hoo!" An owl hooted in a tree. Organ music

began to play, the elaborate, slow, mournful spooky kind that you might hear in an old church, played by an ancient soul so filled with woe that each plunk of the keys and each pipe of the organ reverberates generations of sadness out into the world, a haunting cacophony so mesmerizing you want it to keep going, yet you also cannot wish it to stop soon enough.

The scenery in the ride turned from the forest to castle walls. Thunder and lightning flashed. Red lights and fake flames shot up from the ground, and the buggy twisted through an area with more prison cells. There were skeletons peering out of the doors, and screams coming out from behind them.

Lilac remarked to herself just how very much this looked like the Underworld, where she had been when she was kidnapped. It was uncanny, really, how the likeness of the two were almost exact. Even the animatronic skeletons and spooks on display were so very much like the real demons and creeps she'd seen in the Underworld.

Suddenly, Lilac lost her breath. Those couldn't be real spooks... could they? Her eyes narrowed, and she felt her heart speed up. They looked much too real. She tried to look back and get a better glimpse of them, but the buggy jerked around another corner and through a second set of doors.

They were transported from the dungeon chambers of the Haunted Citadel into the main house. The buggy pulled through a great dining hall, with a table full of spooks sitting down to a feast of toads, worms, gigantic crispy spiders, brains, and skewered bats.

"Bwaahahah!" The voice called out over the ride's speakers. The lights went out, and the buggy stopped. Lilac heard the sound of the riders in the other buggies begin to grumble and complain.

Two fiery demons jumped out of the darkness on either side of the buggy with Hazel, Finn and Lilac inside. They hovered and wove back and forth, an immense heat roaring off of them as they swayed.

All three of the children screamed. And Lilac knew that these were not animatronic bits of scenery. This was not a regular part of the Haunted House.

Lilac took Hazel by the hand and yelled out to her friends, "Come on!"

Hazel grabbed Finn by the arm and Lilac leapt out of the buggy, pulling her friends into action. The riders in the other buggies were muttering to themselves, wondering what was going on in hushed, worried voices.

Lilac let go of Hazel's hand and grabbed the closest object, the pumpkin head of a spook that was sitting at the dining table. She threw it at the nearest fiery figure. The pumpkin was made of foam and was unfortunately much lighter than Lilac had expected. It didn't deter the demon too much. She picked up a wooden chair and threw it, scaring the apparition back a few yards with a crash. People on the ride began to panic, and children started to cry. It was pitch black other than the glowing light from the fiery demons and a few emergency exit beacons tucked into various corners.

Finn picked up a platter of brains and goo from the dining table and threw it at the other spook.

Splat! It went as the flaming figure shirked back.

Lilac pulled the flashlight out of her pocket. She was so relieved she'd taken it, and she reminded herself to never leave home without one again, ever.

"Come on!" She yelled to her friends, and led them bravely into the darkness with her little beam of dim light.

"This way!" Lilac yelled as she ducked down behind a row of knights in armor, each wielding a different massive medieval-looking weapon, swinging aimlessly in the darkness.

The demons approached. Finn shoved over one of the suits of armor and it fell over in a great clatter.

"You'll never leave... alive, that is!" The voice called out from the ride's speaker system.

Lilac shined her flashlight up ahead, leading her friends, all holding hands in a chain through the darkness. People on the ride were screaming, and some were beginning to leave through the emergency exits.

"Were looking for a coffin!" Lilac called back to her friends. "With Dracula!" she led them onwards.

A misty, grey figure popped up and Lilac heard Hazel gasp behind her in horror. Lilac grabbed a candlestick next to the canopy bed and waved it at the grey spook, pushing it back enough so they could pass.

"There it is!" Lilac could see the coffin on the other side of the room. She waved her light towards it.

Suddenly the dim colored lighting of the ride flicked back on, and the buggies started to roll down the track.

"Velcome to the Vampire's Lair!" the silly-sounding vampire voice said over the speakers. Lilac led them over to the coffin and the secret access door.

They all ran through.

"There's that dang kid!" She heard from down the hall to the right.

"Shoot!" she muttered. "This way!" she yelled to her friends and they ran, their shoes squeaking loudly across the tile floor.

Lilac pumped her legs as fast as she could. Hazel and Finn followed, and they were darting back and forth, knocking over tool carts, trash cans, brooms and mops, tipping over buckets of slush water and doing whatever they could to stop the masked men.

"Head 'em off at the aquarium!" Lilac heard the men call into the walkie-talkies.

She rushed past the aquarium and her friends followed around the two corners that would take them to the Sea Pirate's Cove.

The door swung open.

"Right this way, Lilac!" A voice said in a whisper.

"Thanks Roger!" Lilac said as they ran through, and Roger's ghost quickly and quietly closed the door behind them.

"Hide!" Lilac called to her friends.

They looked around in the darkness at the shadowy decorations of the mini golf course. Lilac ran behind the cannon on the far end of the room. Hazel hid behind a giant clam shell. Finn crouched behind the treasure chest. They hid, all three of them still struggling to quiet their panting breath from the fright of the chase.

The door they had entered through began to rattle and bang.

"How'd this get locked?" They heard from behind the door. Then they heard the fumbling rattle of a massive number of keys.

Moments later, the door swung open aggressively.

All three of them held their breath and dared not make a sound.

"Dammit!" One of the masked men yelled, his

footsteps ran down the main ramp into the mini golf course.

"Come on, Phil, I don't think they're in here," another voice called from the doorway.

"We lost 'em. They went back upstairs. They're not in the aquarium, either."

The man named Phil shuffled around the Sea Pirate's Cove, swinging his flashlight dangerously close to the hiding places of Lilac, Hazel, and Finn.

He started back towards the door and then, *thwack.*

"Lord almighty!" the man yelled, hitting the floor with a bang.

"What happened now?" the man from the doorway yelled.

"I musta tripped on something!"

Lilac dared not giggle, but a smile curled onto her lips. Roger must have done something to trip him, she thought.

"We need all hands on deck, upstairs now," Lilac heard over their walkie-talkies, "Thousand dollar bonus to whoever finds those damn kids," the voice said.

"Come on, Phil!" The men hurried out, and the door shut closed behind them.

After a minute, Roger appeared and Lilac popped out.

"Did you figure out a way to shut off the power?"

Lilac whispered to him.

"No, Miss," he shook his head, a bit dejected. "But I've got Mary coming down here to meet us. She said perhaps she can be of help,"

"Mary from the carousel?" Lilac asked.

Roger nodded.

Lilac went over to Hazel and Finn's hiding spots. "Hazel, Finn!" she called. Their heads peeked out from behind the giant clamshell and treasure chest. Lilac lead them over to the spools of electrical wires and cannonballs. "This is Roger, the ghost on the rollercoaster, also known as the caretaker,"

Roger nodded, and Hazel and Finn were looking intently where Lilac was motioning, squinting hard, trying to see the ghost.

"You might have to just kind of let your focus blur out and not try so hard," Lilac suggested. She shrugged. "And you've got to believe."

"Um, Captain Barnabas?" Lilac called out quietly into the large room.

The apparition of Captain Barnabas appeared from one of the porthole windows in the ship.

"Ahoy, Captain Skully!" he called out, "And Captain Melmac, sir, a pleasure as always." He and Roger exchanged a spectral nod, and Barnabas floated through to join them.

"These are my friends, Hazel and Finn," She introduced him to her friends. She felt a little awkward because she wasn't sure if Hazel and Finn would be able to see Captain Barnabas or Roger. "Guys, this is Captain Barnabas," she said.

She looked at them to see what their reaction was.

Hazel's eyebrows were as far up as they could go. Finn's eyes were wide, and there was a twinge of wonder and amazement on his face.

"Oh my god," Hazel said under her breath as she slowly extended her hand. "Are they really there?"

"'Course we is!" Barnabas said with a laugh. "Real as you," he said, "Well, sorta," he corrected himself.

Hazel and Finn continued to stare at the ghosts.

"The legend of the ghost pirate at the mini golf is real!" Finn said, and he looked as if he might almost cry tears of joy, like a kid meeting Santa Claus in person. "And the one on the roller coaster! This is such an honor to meet you!"

"I feel like if I blink, they'll disappear," Hazel said to herself.

"Well I might!" Captain Barnabas said with another laugh.

"Boo!" he called out, his face getting frighteningly serious and then disappearing from in front of them.

"Hey! Where'd he go?" Finn said.

"Hehehe!" The pirate laughed from on top of the crow's nest.

"Okay!" Lilac said, her arms on her hips. "We're running out of time!" She paused. " I was hoping that Roger would be able to just shut off the wiring to the park or do something to power it all down."

"It's not possible," A woman's voice called out, and the ghost from the carousel materialized. "If it was, I'm sure those of us haunting here would have shut it down on many an overcrowded summer day." She laughed.

"Hi, again," Lilac said and the ghost nodded to her.

Hazel and Finn gasped as the mysterious ghost from the carousel joined them.

"Well, " Lilac sighed and looked around at the crew of the living and dead. "The only idea I have, is to run a wire from the top of the Haunted Citadel down to the orb in the old aquarium." She added, "And then get the Lady of the Lighthouse to strike it with lightning." She nodded, although the ridiculousness of the idea made her feel queasy inside. She was suddenly losing her confidence. This all sounded dangerous, and frankly, insane.

But Hazel and Finn nodded at her without hesitation. They stood up one of the big spools of wire to see how maneuverable it was, looking back and forth between each other and communicating in the psychic kind of way that twins often do.

"And these are the cannonballs and the cannon," Lilac said with a sigh, pointing to the obvious cannon behind her. "That was Barnabas's idea. We could break the glass aquarium orb if we had gunpowder, but we don't," she said. That was definitely a flaw in that plan so far, but she thought it would be worth mentioning it just in case.

Lilac looked at her watch. 11:25.

"And we really don't have a lot of time," She got a sick feeling in her stomach and took a deep, uneasy breath to steady herself. "It's almost midnight!" "Oh my god. This is a really harebrained scheme!" she said under her breath, more to herself than her friends.

"Come on, Lilac! You can't give up already!" Finn said. "It's a solid plan, and I think it's gonna work, I think we can do this!"

Hazel nodded back at him, determined under her pink cowboy hat.

"Maybe I can call on the help of some of the spirit visitors out on the boardwalk," Mary suggested, her arms crossed in front of her Victorian dress.

"And Lilac'll give that nasty Astrid hell!" Captain Barnabas called out excitedly.

"Astrid?" Mary said. "Oh, I know her. And that ridiculous rumor that we're sisters!" she scoffed.

"I... I knew you weren't sisters the moment I met you both!" Lilac said, her eyes bright with recognition, a smile appearing on her lips. "Because you're not dressed the same, not at all, you obviously died in... completely different eras."

"Well, you know what else, Little Miss Smarty Pants," Mary said to Lilac in a condescending tone, "I happen know who her sister is! And it's supposed to be a big secret," she said with a bit of a wicked gleam. "Not many people know. But I'll tell you,"

"Who!" Lilac asked in excitement. This had been her mother's dream! To investigate this very ghost and find out who her sister might be! And now, Lilac was going to know!

"The Blue Lady!" Mary said. "Her name's actually Bronwyn. And her sister is Astrid in the Lighthouse."

Lilac gasped a long inhale of disbelief and shock. "I know her..." Lilac said. "I mean I've... I... oh my god..."

"It's true, one-hundred-percent true. I tried to tell this couple of... ghost investigators about it years ago, but they wouldn't listen to me." Mary shook her head and continued talking quickly.

Lilac was taken aback, her brain locked up from realizing that Blue and Astrid were sisters.

"It's a dirty bit of gossip really," Mary continued briskly, "Not polite to talk about it, given the nature of their deaths and all of that. The beautiful blue one pushed the nasty white one off the cliff you know, from what I've heard. And all of that... curse business and jealousy and never-ending rage between the two of them. Too much drama for my taste and I usually don't talk about it. I try to avoid Astrid as much as I can. But," she sighed, "given the circumstances... I thought it might be important for you to know."

"Wh... Why? What? She pushed her off... no..." Lilac said, as her thoughts began to race.

Mary scoffed, her big hat flopping dramatically. "Well, you want to rile her up, don't you? You want Astrid to strike the top of the Citadel? She's not just going to DO that, out of the goodness of her heart— because there isn't any left. You've got to... egg her on! With... with the pain of what haunts her!" She cried out dramatically, her dark swirling eyes locked onto Lilac's.

Lilac shuddered. She felt as if she might throw up again.

"Talk about her sister!" Mary threw her hands up, "And their deaths! Do I have to make it any more obvious, child?"

Lilac hesitated. Tears welled up in her eyes.

"Less than thirty minutes 'till midnight now," Barnabas said, "Better move quick."

Lilac froze.

"You've gotta go, Captain Skully, and fire up the Lady o' the Lightning!" Barnabas said with a grin. "Tell 'er I sent ya!" he added, with a grim chuckle.

"We've got this," Hazel said. "You can do this, Lilac." She hugged Lilac tightly.

Lilac turned around and ran, partly so no one would see her burst into tears, and partly because she was really almost out of time.

She tore through the doors into the crowd of the Fun Park. It was packed with people, kids and adults, both living and dead. The excitement in the air was joyous. More souls had gathered along the beach, waiting for the fireworks show to begin at midnight.

Lilac inhaled deeply— the scent of corn dogs and sweet cotton candy mixed with the salty night air of the seaside was now almost totally overpowered by the unmistakable scent of ghosts. Thousands of them.

She darted this way and that, through the crowd, not looking back to see if there was anyone behind her. She stayed low, crouching behind families, twisting left and right. She saw a mask on the ground and darted to pick it up. It was a simple black kitty cat mask that covered the top half of her face and had ears that stuck up, rather cutely above her head.

Lilac tossed the werewolf mask onto an overflowing trash can and put the cat mask on her head. She continued to run, a wave of confidence growing inside her.

She slipped out of the turnstile at the end of the park. Staying in the shadows and hiding out of sight, running as quietly as she could, into the dark of Halloween night.

16.
LIGHTNING STRIKES

lippity, plippity, plippity plip, her feet ran over the wooden planks of the narrow trestle walkway.

Plippity plip, plippity plip.

The form of the strange older boy jumped out again, from fifteen feet away or so, like an animal, and blocked her path once more.

"You again, huh," he said, "the little ghost hunter girl."

"I'm not a ghost hunter," she said, "and please, let me by. I'm in a hurry."

He stared at her with an intense gaze that made her nervous, like he was trying to read her, to figure her out.

Lilac looked at him in the eye and tried not to show any fear.

"Sorry about your candy apple, kid," he said. "That was a pretty mean trick. But what's Halloween without a couple of tricks?" he laughed.

"Move!" Lilac roared.

"Okay! Okay, jeez!" he said as he flung himself upwards and landed nimbly on the railing of the trestle.

Lilac began to run.

"What are you?" The boy yelled after her.

"I'm just a... little... girl!" she yelled back, but she did not slow down.

She felt the various tools and things in her coat pockets. Wire cutters. Box cutter. A mini flashlight. One plastic spider. An old amulet for good luck and a pale blue stone for protection. There was a folded note with bits about ghost legends that her family had been investigating for generations. And a pack of gumballs. She knew who she was. And she wasn't *just* a little girl. She was Lilac Skully. Defender of Ghosts. Black, Black, and Gremory's worst nightmare. And she was on a mission.

"Well, Happy Halloween, little girl!" he yelled after her. "The key's under the mat if the door's locked."

Lilac barely heard his last sentence as it disappeared into the wind. And she ran, faster than she had ever run in her life. Her legs pumped as hard as they could, up, up, up the switchback trail to the lighthouse.

She ran across the rocky outcropping and across the lawn. Her heart was thumping all the way up to her ears in loud, throbbing beats. Her throat was burning, her breath heaving.

"Astrid!" she called out. "Astrid!"

Whoosh! A massive wave struck the cliff, mere yards away.

She grabbed for the doorknob and rattled it. Locked.

"Under the doormat..." she hesitated, then lifted up the corner of the muddy, ragged woven doormat. There was a shiny silver key underneath. She picked up the key and unlocked the door.

"Astrid!" She screamed into the bottom of the stairs. "Astrid!" she called, her voice echoed up through the lighthouse tower in a frantic cacophony. "It's me! Lilac!"

There was no response.

Boom boom boom boom boom boom boom. Lilac's feet pounded as she went up the stairs.

"Astrid!" Lilac called out. But there was still no reply. When Lilac reached the dark top of the tower, she looked out over the Seaside Fun Park and gasped. The Tilt-O-Scream was tilted sideways—swirling and sputtering with a thick, electrifying green glow all around it. She looked at her watch. 11:54.

"Astri...." Lilac felt her breath stop in a cold chill. Astrid was there, standing right next to her.

Astrid didn't speak, but one of her dark, twisted eyes was half-squinted and fluttering a bit, looking at Lilac as if she'd been caught in the middle of some terrible deed.

"You left your... *litter* up here." Astrid spat at her coldly, nodding to the floor and the white paper bag with the half-eaten candy apple that Lilac had dropped.

"I'm so sorry," Lilac said, picking it up. "I came back here to get it and to apologize and... I need your help," Lilac said to her quietly. "They're sucking up all of the ghosts gathered at the Fun Park," Lilac tried to explain. She pointed to the Tilt-O-Scream, where the unmistakable swirling bluish-green glow of ghosts was beginning to illuminate all around it. "Um, and there's an evil plan, and I need your help to stop Gremory and save the ghosts!"

The woman scoffed. "Help you?" she sneered at Lilac "Save the ghosts?" She whined in a high-pitched, snively voice. "Why would I want to help those... obnoxious merrymakers! And on Halloween night!" She paused, trying to come up with the words to describe her disgust. "Trick-o-treaters and garbage makers," she muttered, pointing to the candy apple bag in Lilac's hand. Her whole face contorted, and the wrinkles wrinkled even more than they had from centuries of contempt and dismay.

"Why, do you know what someone did?" The woman cried to Lilac, not waiting for her response. "Urinated!" She scoffed, utterly horrified. "*Urinated!*" She repeated again, each syllable distinctly.

Lilac looked at her watch.

"In... my... lighthouse!" The apparition began to shake. "Don't get me started on the... dog... *droppings!*" She shrieked and shuddered.

11:55.

"Please!" Lilac cried, "It's not about that, it's just... wrong!" Lilac tried to explain. "They're using the spirits for terrible dark things," Lilac said, although the words stumbled out awkwardly.

"Oh!" The woman's eyes grew wide and sarcastic. "Dark things, you say? Well then. I'll show you dark!"

She growled, her voice getting very deep and gravelly all of a sudden. Thunder and lightning roared above the sea. The eerie mist quickly thickened as black clouds rolled in dense and sudden, obscuring the light of the full moon.

"Y.... Yes!" Lilac said excitedly. "And I need...."

"I don't care what you need!" the woman screamed.

Lilac scurried backwards around the circular walkway. The ghost flew angrily towards her. The sounds of the waves crashed down below and grew in intensity. Lightning flashed and thunder roared again.

"*What about what I need!*" the ghost screamed. Her face contorted to the most horrible, vicious, greedy-looking vile expression that Lilac had ever seen. "Did anyone ever care to think about that?! Ever?!" Astrid screeched.

"I.... I don't know!" Lilac stammered. She looked at her watch.

11:56.

"No!" Astrid howled. Thunder and lightning fired again in the distance, just offshore. Rain began to plop against the windows in random, heavy, and unnervingly slow drops.

Lilac shuddered, unable to speak, the gears of her mind frozen as she tried desperately to get them going and think of a plan. If the Lady of the Lighthouse was not going to cooperate willingly, Lilac would have to come up with another way. She'd have to trick her.

"No one ever asked me if I wanted to spend a thousand years chained to this cliff!" A stroke of lightning flashed even closer.

"No one asked Astrid!" her eyes fumed. Thunder shook the tower, the metal staircase rumbled uneasily.

"No one asked me if I wanted to be.... pushed to my death! So my sister could go gallivanting away with my betrothed... following her heart..." The ghost whined, saying the word, "heart," and fluttering her fingers as if it were the stupidest and most fragile thing she could possibly imagine. "*I was murdered!*" Astrid screamed.

A flash of lightning struck again. Lilac glanced out

and saw the black clouds drawing nearer, obscuring the farthest end of the Fun Park in the distance. But the lightning was not hitting the park or the top of the Haunted Citadel.

Lilac felt a sickening chill rise up from her stomach and into her throat. She thought about what the Carousel Ghost had said. Rile her up. Talk about her sister. And their deaths.

Lilac forced the words out of her voice box, her throat burning and tearing through the cold freeze of panic.

"I know your sister!" Lilac said, as loudly as she could. "I know... Bronwyn," Lilac said.

The woman's eyes pierced Lilac right down to her soul. Lilac wanted to turn away and cry to her mother. Even though she'd never really known her mother, she wished she had, and she wished someone was there to save her at this very moment. But there wasn't.

Lilac looked at her watch.

11:57.

"What?!" The woman said with disgust, as if just by knowing her sister, Lilac was suddenly just as horrible.

"Yes!" Lilac screamed. "Your sister is a friend of mine!"

The ghost gasped, a long, horrible in-breath, as if Lilac were stabbing her in the throat with a sword. The lightning and thunder seemed to slow as the clouds swirled larger and more looming, as if they were in thought.

Lilac wracked her brain.

"And that's not all!" Lilac told her, as loudly as she could, much louder than you normally hear out of Lilac Skully.

"My other friend," Lilac said, not looking away from the hauntingly awful eyes of the ghost. "My other friend," Lilac repeated, "is Captain Barnabas!" She clenched her fists down at her sides. "Barnabas Butkus!"

"Whaaat!" Astrid screamed as lightning struck offshore, three, four, five times in a row, with deafening thunder following a split second after each strike in a pounding roar that all blended together.

"I sunk his ship!" she screamed, "and killed him!" She made lightning strike again, and this time she raised her partly-skeletal hand up in the air and held it over Lilac.

"Nope," Lilac said, folding her trembling arms indignantly.

Although technically, Astrid was correct. She had sunk Captain Barnabas's ship and killed him. Or rather, a shark had killed him. But it was not the time to be agreeable or technical.

"I just saw him, over there," Lilac said, pointing

out towards the Fun Park. "He was sneaking around the Haunted Citadel, up to no good, I heard him say he was planning revenge on you. So I thought you should know." Lilac nodded. That actually sounded quite logical to her.

The ghost let out a bloodcurdling scream. A flurry of lightning strikes clustered off of the coast, and waves smashed against the rocks with furor. The rain began to pound. Lilac hoped there were not too many small crabs and other sea creatures that were being injured or killed by the sudden ferocity of this storm. Lilac looked at her watch. 11:58.

"You mean to tell me," Astrid seethed. "That dreadful... pirate...." She spit the "P" out in pirate as if it were a bug that had been stuck in her teeth. Lilac nodded and nodded, trying to get the ghostly woman to get on with it.

"That dirty pirate!" she said again with another big, spiteful "P," "is right over there?"

"Yes..." Lilac said. "I'm sure of it. And he's got a very nice new ship and everything."

Astrid gasped. "A ship?" She said, one eyebrow raised, and her lips curled up, as if she were already imagining it going down in flames. "A beautiful... ship?" She asked.

"Oh, it's gorgeous, you should see it," Lilac said as

quickly as possible, the seconds ticking down. "And I know how you can get revenge," she said, her eyes narrowing, "before he takes revenge on you!" Lilac's eyes suddenly lit up.

"How?!" Astrid screamed in Lilac's face.

"See that?" Lilac pointed her shaking finger outside to the Tilt-O-Scream, which was now spinning at a blinding speed. The greenish blue glow of ghosts was intensifying around it, and Lilac could almost feel the spark, snap, and eerie hum of Gremory's machine reaching peak intensity, as frightened screams began to pass by on the wind.

Astrid looked out. She looked back at Lilac, and nodded slowly.

"He's wired that up to get *revenge* on you! He's found a way to stop you and your lightning! At the stroke of midnight!"

Astrid's eyes reeled. Thunder and lightning blared so closely, Lilac thought her eyes would be blinded, and her eardrums might pop.

"Just strike the top of the Haunted Citadel with one stroke of lightning," Lilac yelled. "And you'll foil his plans!" She raised both of her arms up dramatically.

A wicked smile came over Astrid's face.

"No!" Astrid screamed at Lilac, her cold, dank, sea-drenched breath hit Lilac with a hair-raising chill.

"N... no?!" Lilac said back to her, stunned and terrified. Lilac began to hear more screams coming from the Fun Park, as the Tilt-O-Scream spun faster and faster, obviously out of control, the sick snap and electrical pulse of it intensified.

"How can I sink his ship if it's not at sea?" Astrid asked Lilac suspiciously.

"This boat is on land!" Lilac tried to explain, knowing there were literally seconds till midnight. She looked at her watch. 11:59 "You'll set it on *fire*!" Lilac cried enthusiastically, as loud as she could, her voice raising, her arms waving up in the air. "You'll burn it to the ground!" She screamed.

Astrid sunk back, her eyes widened.

"You're up to *dirty tricks*, Lilac!" she said in a chilling whisper. "I can feel it!"

Lilac began to shudder. "N... no... I'm trying to warn you!" Lilac looked at her watch again. 11:59.

Astrid's face had frozen. She stared at Lilac. Lilac could hear screams, terrible wailing, and electrical zapping. The pulse of Gremory's machine was reaching full power, and the ghastly green glow of the ghosts getting sucked in was getting brighter by the moment, turning white hot and blinding.

Astrid looked out towards the Fun Park once more. Then she looked at Lilac with a wild glare in her eyes.

Lilac was fairly certain that Astrid would smite her and kill her dead. But Astrid raised one hand to the sea, and in a swoosh, her fingers outstretched—sent a vicious bolt of lightning that hit the very top of the Haunted Citadel.

The flash of the light burned into Lilac's eyes, making it impossible for her to see out of the windows momentarily. She cowered and covered her ears. The shock of it reverberated through the walls and deep into Lilac's soul. She peered at her watch. Midnight.

Lilac looked back out at the Fun Park. The Tilt-O-Scream was sputtering and spinning so violently, Lilac thought it would explode. An orb of ghostly green light surrounded it and began to wobble like its axis had been knocked off center. Sparks of all colors began to shoot out. More terrified screams and shouts erupted in the distance.

There was a loud "bang," then a plume of smoke shot out from the Tilt-O-Scream. The magnificent colored lights of the Fun Park blinked off and on several times, all the way up and down the length of the coast. One, two, three, blinks. Lilac heard more screams wail out on the wind, and then—*poof*.

The Tilt-O-Scream gave off one blinding flash of green light that spun out to white. The greenish glint of ghosts shot out into the night like magical dust. With one more blink, all of the lights at the Fun Park and the entire town of Steamville fell to black. There was a moment of dead silence, and then the distant sounds of chaos and confusion flittered in on the wind.

"Thank you!" Lilac said in shock. "THANK YOU!" Lilac screamed.

Astrid stood proud, her lamp in hand, a poised smile on her lips. "Well, I didn't do it for you," she said, a woeful yet mischievous glint in her eyes. "But after all, it is Halloween. And what's Halloween without a couple of tricks?" She smiled, her mouth and teeth dark and decayed.

"Thank you!" Lilac said again as she squealed and jumped a bit. "Um... I've got to go, but... I promise I'll come back and visit, okay?"

"Hurry back, Lilac," Astrid called to her creepily, "and, Happy Halloween!"

"Happy Halloween!" Lilac said. She ran down the spiral staircase, two steps at a time. She slammed the door of the lighthouse shut and took one shaky breath, and as fast as she could, scrambled down the switchbacks, and over the dark, narrow trestle.

17.
The End

She couldn't believe it! She had done it! The entire town had gone black. Certainly a strike of lightning that huge had been enough to short out all of Gremory's equipment.

Throngs of the living were streaming out of the park, remarking in concerned tones about the lightning and the blackout, and discussing what might've happened with the Tilt-O-Scream. Lilac heard sirens and saw police cars and fire trucks arriving from all directions.

Groups of ghosts were also exiting the park, many of them in tears and recounting terrible tales of being sucked up into thin air, only to be shot back out again over the sky. Some seemed to think it was all part of the night's entertainment. Everything was wet, but the rain had stopped just as suddenly as it began.

Then, Lilac heard her name. It was a familiar voice. But it wasn't Hazel or Finn. It was a ghost. The Blue Lady.

Lilac almost didn't turn around. But she did. Her mouth was curled up, her eyes twisted, and her chin wrinkled. Her fists were clenched. She had been right, and she was about to scream it.

"Lilac, I'm so sorry. You were right," Blue said instantly, the moment Lilac caught her gaze. To Blue's left and right were two of the women Lilac recognized from the Ghost Guard—Minerva, the head librarian, and the elder woman with the crystal staff.

Lilac didn't know what to say.

"I... I know. " She said quietly. "I know. But it's okay." Lilac shrugged. "Because I stopped them. My friends and I did, anyway." Lilac swallowed hard. "We stopped them."

Blue smiled, but just a little.

"Where's Luther?" Lilac asked.

Blue sighed. "He was captured along with several others. It's been a bad night."

Lilac wanted to say, "Ha!" But she stifled it.

The old woman with the staff couldn't contain a wide, knowing grin.

"And, I met your sister tonight." Lilac said calmly to Blue, pointing towards the lighthouse.

"I can explain, Lilac." Blue said solemnly. "We should talk."

"Yeah. We probably should." Lilac said. "But um...

I need to get back to my friends now, maybe we can catch up and talk about it like... some time tomorrow or later?" Lilac said. "I... um... I want to enjoy the rest of my Halloween."

"Come to the community room at the library," Minerva said. "Midnight next."

Lilac beamed. "Okay!" she said. "Um... see you then?"

"See you then," Blue said. "And thank you, Lilac. Happy Halloween."

"Happy Halloween!" Lilac said, as she turned and ran back towards the Fun Park.

Lilac wove through the crowds and back towards the old Sea Pirate's Cove.

Then, *Boom.* It was as deep as the thunder, but just one big boom. And then again. *Boom!*

Lilac looked up. Bright orange and silver fireworks were flying out of the Haunted Citadel. Some people began to cheer, as sparks of black, green, and silver flew in all directions.

Then again, *Boom!* More fireworks flew out of the building, this time in purple and green. Most people oooh'd and aah'd, but some were frightened or seemed unsure.

Boom! She heard again, and *crash!*—the sound of a massive shatter of glass.

More fireworks twirled out everywhere in silver and orange, flying low across the sky.

Lilac pushed through the double doors that led to the mini golf course.

Boom! She heard again, so loudly she felt it in her chest, and she instinctively pulled her hands to her ears. Then a great cheer erupted, a cheer that made Lilac warm to the bone as tears came to her eyes.

It was Hazel and Finn. They were operating the cannon, taking orders from Captain Barnabas. They let a few more cannonballs fly. Lilac had to duck down behind the ship as fireworks shot up and out in every direction.

"Fireworks!" Finn called to her when he saw her. "Fireworks use gunpowder! Woooooo! We plundered some fireworks for the cannon, and we smashed the aquarium tank to smithereens!"

Lilac jumped and cheered. "That's amazing!" she said. "But... we should probably get out of here!" she called to her friends.

They seemed reluctant to stop the cannon, but they ran over.

"We did it! Woo!" they shouted and threw themselves at Lilac for an exuberant group hug of three victorious friends.

"We'll come back and visit, Captain Barnabas!"

Lilac called out to the pirate. "And tell Roger and Mary thanks for us. And thank *you* so much for everything!" Lilac said to him, looking him square in the eye.

"My pleasure, Captain Skully!" He called back and tipped his hat. "See you around, ya darn mini sea-wench," he said, "and yer fine mates, too." He nodded at Hazel and Finn.

"Thanks, Captain!" Hazel and Finn screamed in exuberance.

The children joined the rushing stream of living and dead that were exiting the park.

As the crowds thinned and they rounded up the cliffside bluff, Finn skipped ahead to take the lead, and they ran back to the shrubbery where they'd stashed their bags of candy.

"They're still here!" he said, pulling out the three bags and handing two to the girls. "I told you so!" He ran on, weaving this way and that, cheering and hollering. "Boom!" Finn bellowed with delight. "I can't believe I met real ghosts on Halloween! Woooo!"

"Boom!" Hazel yelled as she jumped and flailed her arms up as much as she could, pretending she was a firework.

"Boom!" screamed Lilac Skully, raising her fist into the air, as a huge smile spread across her face.

She had done it. Black, Black, and Gremory's seaside

plot had been thwarted after all. And she'd made friends. Real living friends. And a few new ghost friends, too.

Lilac dashed through the midnight air, clutching tightly to her giant sack of candy.

"Trick or treat!" Hazel and Finn screamed into the night.

"Trick or treat!" yelled Lilac Skully. "And Happy Halloween!"

A Note from Amy:

Dear Reader, I hope you enjoyed *Lilac Skully and the Halloween Moon!* Halloween is my favorite holiday, and I wanted to give Lilac Skully an unforgettable "first" Halloween experience with her friends. I also loved watching her learn some important things along the way—like how to trust herself, ask for help, and share her feelings—as well as discovering some clues she'll need to rescue her father.

If you'd like to leave a review of this book and share your thoughts with other readers, I would sincerely appreciate it.

Thanks for reading!

Amy Cesari

P.S. Will Lilac's story continue in Book #4?! Of course! You can sign up for Lilac's newsletter and book notifications at LilacSkully.com.

The Lilac Skully Series

About the Author

Amy Cesari is an author and illustrator who lives in an enchanted forest. She enjoys growing pumpkins in the summer, crocheting in the winter, and watching cartoons year-round. She believes in magic and in the power of following your own creativity. And she has every Nintendo game console ever made, plus a vintage Ms. PacMan arcade machine.

You can contact Amy at: amy@lilacskully.com or visit LilacSkully.com for a spooky surprise.

Made in the USA
Middletown, DE
19 November 2018